SHIELDING HIS HEART

NEW YORK TIMES & USA TODAY BESTSELLING AUTHOR
NICOLE BLANCHARD

DEDICATION

For all the introverts
who daydream about bossy men in uniform

GROCERY
BAIT & TACKLE
CLINIC +
GAS
Welcome to Battleboro
est 1902
1. Triple M Ranch
2. Lake County B & B
3. First Baptist
4. Seagram's Bait & Tackle
5. Vet
6. Gas Station
7. Doctor/Pharmacy
8. Lake County Credit Union
9. Eats & Treats
10. Hardware Store
11. Town Hall
12. Fire Station
13. Long Gone Antiques
14. Southern Threads
15. Books & Brews
16. Elementary School
17. High School
18. Grocery Store
19. Post Office
20. Quick Stop

CONTENTS

CHAPTER 1
ALEC

"I thought you said you were coming home today. The girls miss you."

Disappointment. It colors her voice. An all too familiar sound these days. "I'm sorry, Tee. It's double-overtime plus a holiday bonus. I couldn't say no."

Her sigh fills my ears. "You know you don't need to pick up all these extra shifts. We're not hurting for money."

"I know we aren't. I just want to do my part." Our whole marriage had been full of tight spots before her business took off. But just because she's successful doesn't mean I don't want to pull my own weight and do my part. She and the girls are the most important things in the world to me.

Her voice softens, and she says, "We won't. The shop is more successful than ever, and you're making good money. It's okay to slow down every now and then. Enjoy us."

"Why don't I make it up to you, and we take a vacation together? I'll show you how much I enjoy you." It's a pipe dream, at least this month, but I mean it. We don't get away together often enough. As soon as we have time, I'm going to take her back to the same hotel where I first told her I loved her. Lock her in there. And not let her come out until I'm certain she forgives me for working so goddamn much.

She gives a sultry laugh I feel all over. Maybe I shouldn't have signed up for that overtime, damn it. "Oh, really? And how are you gonna do that?"

I whisper filthy things in her ear—all the things I've wanted to do to her but haven't had the chance. And for a little while, it doesn't feel like we have any problems. It feels like it was when we first met. Sure, I'm never home anymore, and we spend more time talking about the kids than naked in bed, but we're still solid. Tana has been the love of my life since the day she planted a kiss on me by the river. She has me as wrapped around her finger as it's possible to be.

I know I don't get to show her as often as I'd like, but she knows how much I love her. I work hard every day to give her and the girls every nice thing they could ask for—and some they don't. A nice house in a good school district, all the pretty clothes their hearts desire, and any stray cat or wild animal our oldest Paisley comes across. Our youngest Gemma is in all the lessons. Karate, guitar, pitching, and horseback riding. She never sticks to one thing long, but she gives each of them her all until she's on to the next. There isn't anything I wouldn't do for them.

"I'm going to hold you to it," Tana says when I finish telling her things that would make my old drill sergeant blush.

"Oh, you can hold it alright." I can practically hear her eyes roll over the phone.

"Miss you," she whispers.

Fuck, man. That's what gets me. Every time. To know how much she wants me there with her. I know she thinks she's being needy when she texts while I'm gone, but I eat it all up, even if I don't tell her that.

I look forward to her constant stream-of-consciousness updates. When she gets busy and doesn't text me every five minutes about something crazy the girls have done or when she asks if I've had any interesting calls at work, I find myself calling her to see what she's up to because I miss her voice.

Yeah, I've got it bad.

"Miss you, too, sweet pea," I say. But I can't help but feel that something's wrong. Something she's not saying. Before I can ask her, the line goes quiet.

The call comes, like so many others, at three a.m. Only this one isn't like any of the others. This call changes everything I thought I knew about my life.

It's a typical night on shift. The bunkroom is quiet as everyone tries to get as much sleep as possible before the next catastrophe. Everyone but me. I can't sleep for shit.

I've got my usual coping techniques: an RPG audiobook I've listened to a hundred times and a daydream about the perfect homestead farmhouse I want to build on my property. I'm thinking about the fencing around that dream home when the tones drop. The very normal sound is followed by a high-pitched sound, a low-pitched sound, and then a feeling of dread.

The speaker blurts out a vague, "Attention EMS and Battleboro first responders. I need you 51 to Highway 278 for a two-vehicle MVC with possible entrapment and ejection from vehicle. LEO is also en route, and bystanders are currently on scene performing CPR on ejected patient."

Within a few minutes, I'm out of the bunk and my sleep pants and jumping into my uniform pants and lacing my boots. All the while doing a mental check of my supplies (sheers, belt, flashlight, knife, window breaking tool, razor to cut seat belts if needed). Our current station has a giant open room with a dozen or so twin bunk beds, and across from me, the three others on shift are doing the same. Our captain, Zeke, is already in the common room.

My partner on shift, Walker, shoots out to the ambulance to get it turned on and the back heated. Keeping a patient warm is almost as important as giving them oxygen. He gets on the phone for the correct address and plots the quickest route to the accident scene. While he's doing that, I get my laptop to record notes on the call, run out the door, and jump in the passenger seat. As he pulls out of the station, I take notes on the laptop and go over information on trauma responses to keep it fresh in my mind.

When I first became a first responder, I was excited about the interesting or unique calls. After being a paramedic for several years, I don't get as amped up because sometimes the calls can be complete bullshit. People often seem to think the ambulance is synonymous with a taxi service. Generally, not the case with an MVC, but you never know what you're going to see when you pull up to a scene.

As we drive, the fire department radios in. "Hey there, EMS. First responders on scene. Yeah, we got two vehicles here. A big ass wreck. Two patients. Possible signal seven."

Signal seven. A fatality. It's gonna be a long night.

We arrive at the intersection, and there are already several police cars pulled to the side of the road with their lights flashing. Walker pulls as close as possible to the vehicle reported to contain the entrapped patient. Med 1, the ambulance with Jax and Remy, pulls next to the ejection, where police officers are already performing CPR on the potential signal seven.

There's never a name attached to the call when we get dispatched. The calls usually include a make, maybe a paint color. In this case, there was neither.

But I don't need that information for my world to start crashing down around me.

Two vehicles—a sedan and a truck—are tangled in a mass of crumpled metal and a shower of shattered glass in the center of the intersection. There are several onlookers along the roadside despite the late hour, and I spot the telltale flash of a camera phone. I've responded to dozens of calls to this intersection, and several people have died over the years. Recently, a teenage boy bound for state college for baseball lost his life in a head-on collision. It's notorious in Lake

County for being a hazard. They've tried to mitigate the dangers with speed bumps and flashing lights at the stop signs, but it never fails that we get several calls a year just for this intersection.

I only see a flash of red and the sliver of a palm tree in the rear window of the sedan, but I know. Walker notices me turn to a statue and looks over as he gets ready to leave the ambulance. "You good, man?"

"They got a name on this patient?" My voice comes out hoarse. It's pitch dark, but there's enough light coming from the emergency vehicles and the truck's headlights tangled with the small car that I can see blood on the dash of the sedan.

It's spattered on what's left of the windshield, too. There are blonde hairs tangled in the glass.

Walker shakes his head and moves closer to get a better look at my face, even though we should both be focused on the patient. "Not yet. Why?"

Beads of sweat coat my upper lip, moistening my words, the salt making me sick to my stomach. "Does that look like Tana's car to you?"

He does a double-take at the sedan only a short distance away. He doesn't seem convinced and looks back over at me. "What?"

"Pull up right fucking next to it." I sweep a hand across my face to get rid of the sweat now streaming down it. I'm gasping for breath and expelling it in heaving shudders. This isn't like me. I'm always in control at a scene. Always. I'm the one who tells the rookies and even sometimes the more experienced guys to keep their cool, take a breath and work the problem. But the more I try to find my sense of calm, the more it spins away from me.

"Are you sure?" Walker asks.

"Yes, I'm fucking sure. Pull the fuck up next to it." My limbs are shaking, and there's a pain in my chest, but I have to focus. If I'm right—and I hope to fuck I'm not—but if I am, she'll need me to keep it together. I have to keep it together.

With one last wary look at me, Walker puts the ambulance into gear. "Yeah, man. Okay."

He whips the ambulance around as fast as he can, and I jump out before it stops moving. I can't seem to get a bead on things. Everything's moving too fast for my thoughts to process, to make sense of it all. The sedan is a red Corolla. Or it used to be before it was T-boned by a black truck. What's left of her car is unrecognizable. It looks more like a UFO than a sedan. Heart in my throat, I race to the site of the collision.

"Get the backboard, the neck brace, and someone find out the ID on the other patient!" At this point, I don't know who I'm shouting at. I'm just praying the person ejected wasn't Tana. It can't be her.

I can't picture a world in which Tana is dead.

I'm the first one to her car. Walker and Zeke follow close on my heels with all the supplies I left behind. The windows are shattered, the driver's side is still intact, and I can see a body through the kaleidoscope of glass on the other side. The tableau is revealed by the flashing strobe lights and jerky flashlight beams from the cops and other firefighters.

"Tana!" I yell, even though the logical part of my brain knows she's probably unconscious. "Tana!"

Zeke comes up behind, places a level hand on my shoulder, and I immediately shrug out of it. "Get ahold of yourself," he says quietly. "Do you need a minute?"

"I need you to get out of my fuckin' face," I growl.

"I don't know what the fuck is going on with you—"

"It's his wife," Walker interjects. "He thinks this is her car."

There's muffled talking following that statement, but I can't hear it over the roaring in my ears. Eventually, someone comes to my side and brushes my hands away from the door. I turn, snarling at the intruder, and then I'm pulled bodily away from the car by the captain.

"You aren't doing her any favors right now, Alec. Let us do our job. We'll get her out." There's a reason Zeke is the captain. Nothing seems to faze him, not even me coming apart at the seams right in front of him. Later, I'll appreciate his stoicism. Now, it makes me want to rage.

"Is she alive?" I bark out to Walker, who has got the driver's side door open. "Is she breathing?" I don't even think about fighting against the captain's hold. All my focus is on Tana's lifeless body.

"We've got a pulse," I hear.

The captain doesn't say anything when my knees go a little weak. They shout her vitals, discuss her various injuries, and for once, my head is completely blank through the chaos.

"Is she alright?" I ask, but I'm not certain anyone can hear me. The din of an accident scene is always overwhelming. The shouts and screams of loved ones or the injured themselves. Barked orders from first responders. Cackles from radios clipped to belts. I'm always able to focus through it all. Always. That's what makes me good at my job. That's why I love what I do. I thrive in the chaos.

"Is she alright?"

Zeke and Walker share another loaded look, and if it wasn't Tana laying there bloody, I woulda had to coldcock one of them for treating me like a patient.

"Goddamn it, someone tell me if she's alright or let me work on her."

Walker grabs me by the arm and pulls me to the front of the car. I fight him every step of the way. "Hold it together, man. Let them do their job."

"Unless you want my fist in your fucking face, you'll tell me how my wife's doing. You know you'd do the same thing if it were Avery." His lips press together at the mention of his girlfriend and the mother of his baby girl.

"Look. She's sustained mild head trauma, potentially resulting in a concussion, but no significant findings of brain injury. She's got a flail chest, probably due to broken ribs. Her vitals are all within normal limits. Pupils are round, reactive, and equal." As he speaks, I keep my eyes on her. They're putting her in a c-collar and spinal package. "Captain wants to fly her out to a level one trauma facility. You can't ride with her, but—"

Before he can answer, I rip away from his hold. "Alec!"

The captain stops me before I can climb back into the ambulance. "You're not going anywhere like this."

"Try and stop me," I snarl.

"Let me give you a ride back to the station, and I'll take you up to County in my truck. You're in no condition to be driving anywhere."

"I'm fine," I say, although I most certainly am not. I can't stomach the thought of being away from Tana, not until I know the extent of her injuries.

"Bullshit," Zeke says quietly, calmly. How he can be so fucking calm, I'll never understand. "Get in the rig. I'll take you back. There's nothing you can do for her going off half-cocked like this, and you know it. Don't argue with me."

Knowing arguing with him will only cost me precious time, I do as he says. The sooner we can get moving, the sooner I'll get to the hospital.

I'm lost in thought during the entire drive back to the station, assaulted by memories of her face behind the window. Bloody. Broken. She'd seemed so small. So fragile.

My hands are sweating. I wipe them on my legs and wonder if the captain is purposefully driving at a snail-like speed to piss me off. He keeps in contact with Med 1, who transports Tana to the helicopter. They make it there success-fully, and she's soon on her way to County Hospital, an hour drive away but a short twenty-minute flight. Because of the broken ribs and possible head trauma, it's safer to fly her by helicopter than transport her by ambulance.

Zeke is quiet for most of the drive to the hospital. What can he say? Not a damn thing. He relays each update. When they take off. When they land. After that, there's not much we'll know until we arrive at the hospital. Which seems to take an eternity.

When we arrive, I'm out the door and at the emergency desk like a shot. When I get a nurse, I say, "I'm Alec Dorran. My wife Tana was in an MVA. She was just brought here by chopper."

The rest is a blur. She's in critical condition and in the ICU. Someone leads me to her room, where I see her through a small window, hooked up to monitors and covered in stark white bandages.

There's only one thing that sticks out from the litany of information the doctor spits out at me.

"We won't know the extent of her injuries until she wakes up."

What could be worse than this? I wonder.

Please wake up. Please.

I fall asleep holding her hand and hoping I'll see her eyes again in the morning.

Please come back to me.

I can't lose you.

CHAPTER 2
TANA

He comes around the doorway, his face lifted in hope.

Which I've come to recognize after four weeks of the same routine. And like always, when my own expression doesn't brighten at his appearance, he tries to mask the disappointment with measured politeness. "Hey, Tee."

He's said the same thing every time he's come to see me. *"Hey, Tee."*

Like if he says it enough, maybe I'll get used to the routine. To seeing him like this. To everything that's insane and unfair and *wrong* about my life. Like if he calls me by a nickname, it'll make our relationship seem more real.

Nothing about my life seems real right now.

His gaze shifts to the nurse at my side. I scowl because I don't even remember her name, and I know she's told me a thousand times. Details of my day-to-day life still slip away from me from time to time if I don't write them down, leave myself a note on the phone I was given, or repeat them over and over in my mind. It could be worse, I've been told. I could be in a coma, in a vegetative state, or dead.

But none of that consoles me.

I almost think it would be better. Easier to be any of the above. At least I wouldn't be in this constant in-between state.

With continuous reminders in the form of these visits.

I don't respond because I don't know what to say. Seeing him makes me feel awkward, which makes me irrationally angry. I pick at the threadbare sheets wrapped around my waist. My head begins to throb, and I wonder if it will be long before my next dose of pain medication. I'm not even certain if I've had it yet or not, but at least it dulls the edges of my thoughts a little instead of feeling the steady maelstrom of confusion, worry, and anger. I'm so tired of thinking.

"You look beautiful today." *Liar.* But he says that every time despite the purple-dark bruises on my face and the gash on my forehead. I've studied the face in the mirror in my hospital room a thousand times, trying to imagine what he sees that has him coming back day after day.

Aside from the bruises and bandages and the gigantic gash on my forehead, I don't see anything special. Flat blue-gray eyes and dark blonde hair in need of a trim and a style that isn't hospital bedhead. A slightly stubby nose, and okay, maybe I have nice lips. But is that worth this amount of dedication?

He edges a hip onto the chair by my side. It probably has an indent molded to the shape of his ass at this point. "Have you had a good day so far? It's a pretty afternoon if you want to go outside for a walk."

I don't want to, not with him. But I haven't seen the sky all day, so it's tempting. I waffle between denying him or myself and begrudgingly get to my feet. He tries to help me to the wheelchair, but I collapse into it all on my own. Angrily, I wheel myself out of the room with him following close behind.

"When can I leave this place?" I hate that I have to ask. I should be allowed to go whenever I damn well please. I shouldn't need anyone's permission.

"We're going outside now."

I stifle the urge to yell. I may not know a lot about what's happening, but I know acting irrationally won't do me any favors. "I mean for good. I feel fine."

"The doctors say you may need a little more time to heal. We'll know more after we meet with Dr. Rennen this afternoon. It's this way," he gently corrects when I turn down a hall I was certain leads to the elevators.

He doesn't comment when I turn around and wheel past him. "I feel *fine*," I reiterate, but there isn't as much power behind the words, no matter how loud I say them.

Silence fills the space between us on the elevator ride to the first floor. The lobby area is empty, and I work up a sweat slapping at the wheelchair until the automatic doors slide open and a fresh breeze hits my skin. I turn my face up to the sky, letting the soft afternoon sunlight warm me from the outside in. I imagine it purifying me of the hospital stench.

As soon as I get out of here, I'm going to spend an entire day outside. No monitors. No people. No medicine, bad food, or stupid TV—just me, the outdoors, the wide-open sky, and the sun on my face.

Maybe I'll even camp somewhere, just for a while. The last thing I want to do when I'm well enough to leave is spend more time cloistered away inside four walls and a roof.

"The girls made you some drawings. Do you want to see them?"

There's that hope again.

"Okay," I answer without opening my eyes.

"I'm going to put them on your lap," he says. I try to focus on finding zen with the sun and the breeze, but it isn't as easy when he gets close to me. It's probably the injuries. A couple broken ribs, one hell of a concussion, and a bruised lung would make it hard for anyone to breathe. But curiously, this reaction only happens when *he's* around. My head goes a little light, and my chest aches like I'm about to cry, but I never do. And I don't know why.

I hear paper rustling, a soft whisper next to my head, and his hand brushes against my thighs. The thin pants and shirt that have become my daily uniform do little to protect me from his heat. I'm thankful I'm not hooked up to the monitors anymore because my heart skips a little in my chest, and my calm breathing falters. I pray he doesn't notice, but he's already drawing away to give me space.

Opening my eyes, I blink away the floating dots from the

sun, and my gaze lands on the drawings on my lap. Then I'm blinking my eyes for entirely different reasons. The girls have painted two family portraits for me. One is a mess of blotches and scribbles. The other is more studied, with a clear knack for art. They've both painted four people. Alec and me. The two of them in front.

My voice is hoarse when I find it again. "Tell them thank you for me."

"I will, but you can tell them in person. If you want."

I shake my head. "I don't want them to see me like this."

"We've been meeting with a child psychologist, explaining to them about the accident. They both understand, and Dr. Teatree seems to think it would be a good idea for them to see you."

But what about me?

The thought is selfish and instantaneous. Would it be a good idea for me? Could I handle seeing them?

"I don't know. I still look like I've been hit by a car." The joke lands flat, which is shocking because Alec always seems to know what to say. He glances away from me, his lips firming into a line. I feel a little bad, but not really. I'm the one with broken ribs and a busted face. I'm a mass of bruises, and the only thing holding me together is the mood stabilizers. Is that really what I want to subject two little girls to? They deserve a mother who's whole. They deserve the mother they had before the accident.

"Think about it," he urges after a while, though he's still not looking directly at me. It's almost like it hurts him to see me. Maybe it does. "It could help. I could bring them here—"

"No, I don't want them at the hospital." Maybe my tone is harsh, but apparently, he needs me to be firm to get the point across. "I'll see them, but not here. Not like this. When I'm better, and they let me go."

I don't know what it is about me, but I have this talent for shutting down even the most innocuous conversations these days. Mentally, I shrug my shoulders because I know, in this case, I'm right. And if the result is that he lets me enjoy the afternoon in silence, even better. Apparently, post-accident Tana is a real bitch.

"I understand," he says softly, finally. "I'm sorry for pushing you."

And then I feel like crap, so I look away from him. I wish he'd stop being so goddamn nice to me all the time. Especially when I don't feel like I've done anything to deserve it.

The quiet is back, but at least we're outside where it feels like I have room to breathe. To be. After a time, Alec begins pushing the wheelchair through the hospital courtyard, and I don't protest because the change of scenery is so, *so* welcome. Hopefully soon, I'll get to see more than this courtyard.

"I'll take you back up. It's time to see Dr. Rennen," Alec says after a while.

I nod silently, and neither of us says anything else as he wheels me back up to my room.

I've liked the doctor from the moment I met him. He's the one point of calm in my day where I feel like someone knows what the hell is going on. That's why it pains me to want to wring his neck.

"What do you mean it may never come back?"

I try for a calm voice but don't manage it. At all. Anger and disappointment make my voice quaver pitifully. Hot tears threaten, but I blink them away. I won't cry anymore. I won't.

Dr. Rennen sits at my bedside and meets my gaze. "I'm sorry, Tana. I wish I had better news. I'd hoped your memory would return within the first few weeks after the accident. It still can, but there are rare cases when it never returns. I know we've spoken about how you may remember some of your childhood memories and early adulthood. It's the more recent memories you've lost. You'll have difficulty retaining new information for a time, but I have every confidence that with therapy, you can live a normal, healthy life."

"So I can remember how to do multiplication and tie my shoes or ride a bike, but I can't remember the man I'm married to or the children I gave birth to?"

The doctor takes off his glasses and cleans them with the side of his coat. "It's not fair. I'm sorry."

For some reason—I don't know why—I glance up at Alec, who has gone sheet-white. The urge to take his hand overwhelms me, so I grip the material beside my thighs.

"Are you saying she may never get her memories back?"

Alec's voice is much steadier than mine, even if he looks like he's going to be sick.

"The brain is a mysterious thing, but I can't tell you with certainty if she will. Her short-term memory will improve with time, and she'll need to continue her therapy to improve her fine motor skills. But that doesn't mean she won't otherwise recover physically. I fully expect to see her running circles around us by next spring."

Should I miss the woman I used to be? The one everyone seems to know? I don't know how to feel about this news. A part of me hoped I'd wake up one day with the answers to all the questions in Alec's eyes. But then there's a part of me bursting in anger at how all of his *hope* must have known, deep down, that there wasn't any. The woman he loved may as well have died, and he's stuck with me.

A stranger.

I swallow hard. "When will I be released from the hospital?"

"Provided you have somewhere to go and someone to help you to and from appointments and help you transition, I don't see why you couldn't be released today," Dr. Rennen says in a helpful voice.

My shoulders droop. I don't even know if I have anyone —anyone other than Alec. "I—"

"Of course she does," Alec says and takes a step closer to me. He's got some of his color back now. "She's coming home with us."

"I don't want to be a burden," I start.

Alec pays me no mind. "You'll let me know about her

appointments and therapy. Is there anything I can do at home to make her comfortable?"

The conversation fades under the sound of buzzing in my ears. I want to speak up, to object, but I realize with growing horror that I have no one else. No one has come to see me aside from Alec. I don't even know if I have family outside of him and his girls. My girls. Or any friends to speak of. Besides, how could I ask anyone to take me on when I don't know what the past holds for me, let alone the future?

CHAPTER 3
ALEC

Dr. Rennen leaves, and I collapse into a chair, rubbing a hand over my face and feeling the scruff there. I'm in desperate need of a shave, but I don't think I've slept in the weeks since Tana's accident, let alone had time to groom myself properly.

I keep replaying our last conversation in my head, wondering if I'd said something different or done something different, could I have saved us both from all of this? Would she have been at that intersection if I'd turned down working that extra shift like she'd asked? I should have been there taking care of them. It should have been me. Tana was the glue that held our family together.

"You don't have to do this." The words spoken come from the voice of the woman I love but a stranger's mouth, pulling me away from my misery. I don't know which is worse, knowing I may never get the love of my life back or seeing her right in front of me, but having her be hopelessly out of reach.

Meeting her gaze, I say, "Do what?" I'm too tired for this.

"Take care of me."

It's barely a whisper, and I can tell she hates the thought of being helpless, beholden. I almost laugh. The person sitting in front of me couldn't be more different from the woman I married. Tana loved to have other people take care of her, but not in a malicious way. She grew up without a family, with no one else to rely on. When we started dating, it was one of the things that attracted me to her the most. I liked taking care of her, and she ate it up. There weren't many women who enjoyed that from a man, but she did. And it worked for us. She took care of me right back, but in other ways. We fit each other. So, where do we fit now? Where do we go from here?

I heave a sigh, wondering if the vows I made to this woman still apply now that she can't remember them. She may have the same eyes I've looked into a million times, the same lips I've kissed and memorized, and the same voice I've heard in a thousand different ways. But this woman? This isn't my wife.

At the same time, I can't let her go. Somewhere, somewhere inside of her is the woman I love. The woman I've promised to take care of in sickness and in health.

What kind of man would I be if I gave up on her now?

Not the kind who could look at their reflection in the mirror, that's for damn sure.

"Of course, I'm going to take care of you." I want to say,

"You're my wife," but that doesn't feel right. She shrinks away whenever I get close. She looks at me like a stranger, and hell, I am to her. Could the woman I loved just be gone? Just like that? One moment I have everything, and the next, it's taken from me. The thought occurs to me that it would have been easier if she'd died, but it makes me sick to my stomach to even think it.

"Just until I figure out what I'm doing next. Just for a little while." I don't know if she's saying it to herself or me, but maybe we both need to hear it.

"I'll call my mother and tell her to let the girls know you're coming home." Her eyes widen, and I'm close enough to see the pulse jump in her throat, so I add, "Unless that's too much for you."

There's a pause while she tries to think of an excuse. Not finding any, she says, "No, I understand. They want to see their mom."

"And they understand their mom isn't well right now. At least as well as kids can understand. I shouldn't have pushed you before."

She picks at the thin hospital sheet and doesn't meet my eyes. "You don't have to apologize. You're trying to do what's best for them as a father. I'm sorry for being difficult."

"I'd say you weren't, but that would be a lie." Her gaze lifts to mine, rebuttal already on her tongue when she sees my wry smile and laughs.

"Ha, ha. Very funny. You shouldn't tease the invalid."

It feels so fucking good to hear her laugh. My eyes slip close for a moment, and I soak it in. I never thought I'd hear it again. It soothes the raw, worried parts inside me, at least for a little while.

"I think we both know you're anything but disabled. You wouldn't be getting sprung from this place in a little over a month if you weren't a fighter." That, at least, the old and the new Tana have in common. She may have been sweet, kind, and thoughtful, but she had a backbone of steel. It makes me wonder what other things they'll have in common. Is it strange I've started thinking of the two of them as completely different people?

I push to my feet because worrying about it hasn't done any good over the last month. According to Dr. Rennen, it may even be permanent, so there's no amount of worrying that'll change a damn thing anyway. "I'll see what discharge paperwork we need to take care of."

She opens her mouth and pauses.

"What?" I ask.

"Do you mind if I take a shower? Change my clothes? All I have is this." She fingers the pajama outfit the girls had picked out.

I laugh a little. "Yeah, of course. I brought a suitcase of your clothes. I'll get it from the closet."

Retrieving it from her, the scent of Tana's perfume wafts up from the fabric, and my throat closes. She doesn't notice as I pass them over to her.

"I'll only be a minute," she promises.

"Take your time," I murmur.

CHAPTER 4
TANA

When I come out of the bathroom, he's waiting for me with his head slumped in his hands. He looks up when I clear my throat. God, he looks so tired. Worn slap out. I feel a stab of empathy.

It's not his fault that I'm here. It's not anyone's fault besides the person who hit me. But they are dead, and I have no one else to blame. No one else I even know. He's the only person I recognize in my strange new life aside from the nurses and doctors who tend to me. Others came to visit, but I've already forgotten their names. Friends, neighbors. Alec's coworkers.

He seems so determined to bring the before-me back, and I'm mad as hell about it. What if she never comes back? What if all he has left is *this* me? What if the after-me isn't someone he likes? What if I get used to him and lean on him, and then all of it is ripped away when he realizes I'm not and can't be the woman he fell in love with?

So when he gets his feet and takes a step toward me, I take one in retreat. I can't risk it. I may act like a bitch and pretend to be strong, but inside I'm not. Inside, I'm as beat up and tender and broken as my good-for-nothing brain.

This new world is scary and unfamiliar. I recognize nothing. I know nothing. The only thing I'm sure of at all is that it can be taken away in a second. So until I'm certain what I'm going to do, I can only rely on myself. Trust only me.

Alec's face falls at my retreat, and he quickly wipes the expression away. It's moments like this when I know I hurt him that I doubt my plan to keep my distance. But I know it'll be better for both of us in the long run. I don't know how I'll do that with his—our—children, but I'll figure it out.

"I'll pull the car around to the entrance." His expression is shuttered, and he sticks his hands in his pockets.

I wrap my arms around my waist and nod. "Thank you. I'll meet you down there."

He shakes his head. "I'll come back up and get you."

My chin goes up. "I can manage. You can't keep treating me like I'm glass."

"Right." He looks like he wants to argue, but he doesn't push it. "I'll get the car."

"Thanks." I wait until he's out of the room before I relax.

It would be so much easier if the body I'm inhabiting didn't respond so strongly to him. Again, thank God I'm not hooked up to the monitors anymore, so my reaction isn't on display for the whole room to see. In the beginning, they wrote it off as fear or nerves, but I know the truth. Which I will never share. Whenever Alec gets close to me, I feel it down to my soul. The sensitive parts of me tingle and come to life. My brain may be damaged, but my body isn't. And it knows him. Knows him better than I know myself at this point.

It's infuriating to respond to him and not really know why or have any control over it. There's a history there I don't recall. He knows it, and my own body knows it, but my brain is the problem.

Whenever he gets close to me, I want to let him fold me into his arms. I want to surrender to his comfort. And that's what scares me. Because although I should trust him, all I can think about is that I don't really know him.

All I know is what I've been told or learned through eavesdropping when everyone else thought I was asleep.

One, his name is Alec Phineas Dorran.

Two, my name is Tana Markham-Dorran.

Three, we have two children named Paisley and Gemma.

Four, we've been married for over ten years.

Five, we've known each other most of our lives and started dating in our early twenties.

Six, he served four years in the Army until he was medically discharged.

Seven, he is, without a doubt, the sexiest man I've ever seen. This isn't saying much because the total of my memory is limited to the time I've spent in the hospital. But I have a feeling even if I traveled around the world and actually remembered it, he would still be the sexiest man I've ever seen. Keeping my distance from him will be incredibly hard when all my body wants to do is make friends with him.

Now that he's gone and I'm alone, I think back to the earliest memory I have of him. I had woken up from a drug-induced slumber or coma, and he was leaning over my bed, holding my hand with one of his while the other was stroking my hair. He was so damn beautiful I wasn't even scared at first. But even if I was terrified, the soothing words he whispered would have put me immediately at ease. His eyes were locked onto mine, and when he realized I was awake, they filled with a sheen of tears. Before I realized what was happening, I put my hand to his cheek.

Then he said a name. And that's when I realized something was wrong because I asked, "Who is Tana?"

He gave me this look. At first, it was like he didn't understand what I meant. Then the realization dawned for him and for me. I realized I was supposed to be Tana, and he realized the woman he loved didn't remember who she was.

He held onto me for a moment longer. As the confusion set in for me, I pulled away.

I didn't know this man. I didn't even know myself.

I'd give anything to go back to that split second when I had just awoken and didn't realize what was going on. The split second when he had me in his arms, and I felt at peace with the world. At home. For that one moment, I knew where I belonged. I haven't felt that way since.

The real fear is that I'll never feel like that again.

It's difficult to get down to the first floor without a wheelchair. I have to waive liability to the hospital, but I'm determined to walk out of this place on my own two feet. I've been doing over a month's worth of physical therapy to walk again. And I'm determined not to rely on anyone else whenever I can. Besides, I'm lucky to even be able to walk. They weren't sure I would when I woke up.

Alec is waiting at the hospital's exit. He's annoyingly reliable. There must be a catch, right? No one can be that good of a person and be so good-looking. Truthfully, it's unfair.

From the top of his thick tawny hair to the bottom of his strong feet, he's perfect. He hadn't been wearing shoes that first night. Long after we went through the back and forth with doctors about the amnesia, he finally fell asleep in the chair next to me with his feet crossed at the ankles and propped up over the side. For the record, he's also adorable when he sleeps.

Neither of us says anything as he loads my bags up into the back of the truck. I keep my mouth shut as he opens the door and helps me inside. I'm afraid if I speak, all my fears and insecurities will come bursting out. It's better to say nothing.

I roll down the window to feel the breeze on my face as he pulls out of the hospital parking lot. I'm giddy with excitement and nerves and fear. Everything about this is new. It's scary and thrilling, and it makes my heart pump wildly in my chest. Not just because I'm in close quarters with Alec, but because I don't recognize any of my surroundings.

Ravaged. That's the only word I can think of to describe the landscape around me. It certainly doesn't resemble the town I grew up in. It's almost like a giant swiped his hand over the trees and buildings we drive by. The trees are broken a few feet up from the base. Buildings are leveled or are in different states of repair or disrepair. Blue tarps flap over many of the roofs.

"Hurricane Michael hit in 2018. It was a Category 5 and destroyed pretty much most of the area. Battleboro is still recovering," Alec says when he notices my awestruck expression.

"But it's 2022, isn't it?" I can't help but ask.

He gives me a wry grin that makes the corners of his eyes wrinkle up attractively. Damn him and the fact that even wrinkles make him look hot.

"If you think this looks bad, you should've seen it right after. They've done a lot of work since, but the truth is, it'll be decades before it even looks anything remotely normal."

I feel a lot like the destroyed landscape around me. A ghost of my former self. Never able to be restored to what it once had been.

Tears prick the back of my eyes, and I keep facing the window so Alec can't see me cry. I haven't done much crying since the first week. But getting out of the hospital and facing the fact that I have no idea who I am, who the people in my life are, or even where I'm from hits me all over again.

How am I supposed to cope with this? What's the right thing to do? How do I even begin?

Not to mention all the people who knew the before-me. Like Gemma and Paisley. According to him, I even owned my own business. I must have had people who worked with me, customers. How do I deal with all the things they want from me? How do I face their constant disappointment when I'm not who they think I am or want me to be?

I almost beg Alec to drop me off somewhere. Then I remember I don't know if I have any money. I don't even know where I would ask him to take me. A hotel? That's not a feasible solution. I won't be able to get a job until physical therapy is over. What would I even do? Do I have any skills? My memory is shot. It will also be a while before I can go out in public because of the still-healing bruises and bandages covering my sutures. It's hopeless.

The truck stops, shocking me out of my spiral of self-deprecation. I glance through the front windshield and find a cute little two-story brick house in front of us. There's a two-car garage at the end of the driveway, a small, covered porch, and a bright blue door.

That little detail is enough to distract me, at least for now. Alec doesn't seem like the type to have a bright blue door. He's more of a no-frills kind of guy. I realize with a jolt that his wife probably picked the color. Probably bullied him into it. Then another jolt. His wife was me.

I start breathing rapidly. I've been aware of the reality that we are married. But it's not until I see the door that all the implications hit me. I'm going to walk into a house full of these little details of a life together. Pictures, videos, children. It almost makes me want to ask him to take me back to the hospital.

But then he's getting out of the truck and opening my door. I don't know why the action makes my heart go all soft, but I don't argue with him, which surprises him too as I take his hand and let him help me down. Thankfully, he doesn't comment on it and simply gets one of my bags from the back of the truck.

I'm frozen in the same spot where he left me when he puts a hand on my lower back.

It shocks me enough to step toward the house, my eyes catching a quick flutter of the curtains in the front window. Despite my fear and my nerves, it makes me smile. It's a sad smile, but it distracts me from the feel of Alec's hand on the sliver of skin between my shirt and jeans. Two little girls peer out from a thin slit in the curtains.

I don't know what I expected to feel when I saw them for the first time, but all I feel is apprehension. The only thing I remember about children is being one myself—and even that isn't a perfect recollection. These girls deserve so much more than a broken person. They deserve the mother who grew them and gave life to them. Who raised them and loved them.

I reach for Alec's hand as he tries to move around me with my bags. He stops and looks back with a lifted eyebrow. "What's wrong?"

"What do I say?"

Alec glances back at the curtains, and we both watch the girls duck out of sight. "Be honest. They may be young, but they're smart kids. We've talked a lot to them about what happened and how you won't remember them."

When I still don't move, he turns toward me. I hesitate, then say, "I don't wanna hurt them. They're just kids."

"Let me worry about all of that. All they care about is

seeing you and that you get better. You may not know them, but they know you and love you very much. All I ask is that you don't make any promises and treat them with kindness."

I blow out a long breath. I don't even know if I'm good with children. But I can handle those two things. Before I can forget, I take out my phone and jot down those requests in the notes app.

"All right," I say and follow him up the short walkway to the porch.

He opens the door, and I'm met with the scent of apples and cinnamon. Like someone just baked a fresh apple pie, which couldn't be more fitting, really. From what I've learned so far, Alec and his family seem to be the perfect American pie family. Like the ones I've seen on countless television commercials. The kind of life and family little girls dream of. It smells like what I imagine a home would smell like, and even though this is technically my home, it causes a little hitch in my stomach when I realize it doesn't feel that way.

Is it possible to be jealous of yourself? Because I am. Intensely. Especially when Alec stands by his two daughters, and they all turn and look at me. I want to belong to them. Somehow knowing that I used to makes it worse.

"Hello," I say steadily as I can. My hand tightens around my phone, and it bites into my palm. "You must be Gemma," I address the taller one. "And you must be Paisley," I say to the smaller. "I've heard a lot about you."

The first girl frowns and narrows her brown eyes at me. "No, I'm Paisley," and then points to her younger sister, "and this is Gemma."

Gemma giggles. "Hi," she whispers shyly.

I give them a small smile. "I know. I was just joking with you. Your dad showed me pictures. I'm really sorry for everything that's happened."

Gemma has a hold of Alec's hand, and Paisley stands nearby. Paisley's not as trusting and lighthearted as her sister. I wonder how I can tell that already. Maybe because she reminds me a lot of me. And then my heart cracks open when I realize she looks like me too.

Both girls have my blonde hair color, but that's all the sisters have in common. Gemma looks like her father. The same square-shaped head, the same wide, full lips. Even their eyes, almond-shaped and a warm honey brown, match.

Paisley has my somewhat deep-set, hooded eyes that are an identical pale, almost gray, blue. The same thin mouth. And her facial structure is longer and leaner than her sister's.

And while Gemma may look completely different, she has the same beauty mark on her right lower cheek that I do.

Like everything else, it's strange to see myself reflected in their faces and not know them.

CHAPTER 5
ALEC

I rest a hand on Paisley's shoulder. She gazes at Tana with trepidation and a little resentment. On the other hand, Gemma is smiling her huge, gap-toothed smile. I knew when Tana was in the accident, it wasn't necessarily Gemma I'd have to worry about. That girl is basically made of rubber. Everything bounces off her.

But Paisley. . . Paisley, I knew, would require more careful handling.

"You don't remember anything?" Paisley asked with her characteristic bluntness.

Tana's hand clutches the strap of her bag. Her eyes flit around her surroundings. "Not much about myself. Your dad told me to be honest, so I'm happy to answer any questions. I remember how to do things most of the time. Like brushing my teeth or doing algebra or things like that. But not most of the more important stuff. I don't remember my family. I don't remember me. I don't even know what kind of movies I like or my favorite food." She glosses over mentioning the girls. I don't blame her. I couldn't imagine not knowing them. If Tana is half of my heart, our girls are the other half.

I swallow hard. I've been so caught up by what I lost—everything—that it hadn't occurred to me, not really, that she lost everything too. My hand tightens on Paisley's shoulder. More out of reflex than reproach.

Paisley doesn't seem to notice. She's focused intensely on Tana. "Do you want a tour of the house?" Paisley offers. I release a breath I didn't know I was holding. Honestly, their meeting could've gone either way. It seems as though Paisley is willing to be on her best behavior. Which is more than I could've hoped for.

Gemma loves this idea. She bounces up and down, eyes bright, and goes to Tana's side to take her free hand. "Yes! Let's take a tour. Come on, come on, I'll show you my room."

I meet Tana's eyes before Gemma can drag her from the room. I mouth, "Is that okay?"

Tana merely nods and allows Gemma to drag her up the stairs to where the girls' rooms are. Paisley follows cautiously behind and gives me a small smile. It reassures me a little, but I know this may just be the calm before the storm.

While the girls show Tana their respective bedrooms and, I'm sure, regale her with as many memories as they can recall–Gemma in particular—I retrieve the rest of Tana's things from the truck. I want to put them in our bedroom. I find myself moving in that direction, then abruptly stop. It's the place I've missed her the most. I've woken up every morning since she's been gone reaching for her. She always takes up too much of the bed. Steals the covers. And though she'd never admit it, she snores. But goddamn, I'd give anything to be cold, smothered, and kept awake because she sounds like a buzz saw. I truly didn't know what I had until it was gone. My heart aches, and I spin around, forcing myself to think of anything else.

I bring her things to the spare room just off the kitchen in the back of the house. It used to be her craft room, where she would make the girls matching shirts for our Disney trips. She would wrap ribbon to make elaborate bows for their hair or customize birthday cards for her friends. Tana had a way of making the ordinary moments in our lives extraordinary. The little crafts she would do for the girls when they were small had become a lucrative business in the past few years. She sold her creations online to the point where the side hustle became a success. I couldn't have been prouder.

But now, all her supplies are boxed up in big Rubbermaid storage bins. Her paper and glitter and ribbon and blank T-shirts. The machines that worked whatever magic they did. All that stuff is now stored in the attic waiting for her to use them again. Waiting for her to remember.

Like the rest of us.

My mom cleaned out the room and carefully boxed everything up. I didn't say it to her, but I think she knew I couldn't bear to pack away Tana's things. She'd given us a spare bed from their house and dressed it with a matching floral quilt and shams. It was the color of sunshine and soft grass. The punches of green and yellow tied into the curtains and a small rug at the foot of the bed. It was homey and warm and inviting.

And I hated it.

I hated that she would be in this room so close to me and yet so far away.

I took my time unpacking her clothes, putting them in the dresser, and hanging them in the closet. The ritual was surprisingly soothing. She may not have my wife's memories, but she still smelled like her. The same clean, feminine scent without perfume or other adornments. It reminded me that she was in there somewhere. The essence of the woman I loved was there.

That's all that mattered.

Soon, I heard footsteps coming down the stairs. With the clothes and other things unpacked, I went out into the kitchen and found them standing around the generous island.

This is where I feel Tana the most in our home, aside from our bedroom. She loved to cook. If cooking were a love language, I'm pretty sure it would be hers. Along with the crafts she would make for people for any given holiday, she would also bake or cook them something to go along with it. When her parents passed away and left her a small life insurance policy, she used it to renovate our kitchen into her dream kitchen.

I heard or read somewhere that the kitchen was the heart of the home. I found that true now more than ever, having Tana back in it. Because she is the heart of our family.

She'd been determined to have restaurant-grade everything—the stove, the oven, the dishwasher, even the sink. Most of my favorite memories of our family are in this kitchen, with Tana at the stove and the scent of something delicious lingering in the air.

The house feels empty now, like the kitchen has been since she's been gone.

She stands next to the sink as Gemma describes her favorite dinner.

"Do you like spaghetti?" Gemma asks, her high-pitched voice full of excitement. I should've known she'd be thrilled at the thought of food. At eight, she eats like a line-backer and is still willow thin.

Tana shifts from one foot to another and gnaws on her lower lip. "Honestly, I'm not sure."

Paisley's watchful eyes slide from Tana to me. "You used to make it all the time," she says in a voice that isn't accusing or resentful but somewhere in between.

It's like a sucker punch. My little girl can't believe she's looking at her mother, who doesn't remember something they used to do every week. Something as ingrained in her core memories as Tana's scent is in mine.

It occurs to me then that this could've been a terrible idea. What if this completely screws them up more than they already are? Maybe I should've found somewhere else for Tana to stay until we figure things out more. The girls have been so excited, but they're children. They need me to protect them from the harsh realities of the world.

I'm about to recommend that they give us some space

when Tana rests her elbows on the island and leans conspiratorially closer. "Well, I guess the only way we're going to find out is if we make some. Do either of you know how to make spaghetti?"

Paisley's shoulders relax a little. Spaghetti is her favorite. But everything in me tenses up. The smile on Tana's face and the soft, somewhat mischievous tilt of her lips made me fall in love with her.

Gemma squeals with glee. "Yes, you let us help you all the time."

"Gemma," I say warningly.

"No, she didn't. But we can tell you how to make it," Paisley says and nudges her sister with her shoulder. "Remember what Dad said. No lying to Mom, especially about stuff she can't remember."

I let out a breath. So far, so good. The jury is still out on whether we've screwed them up. I'm sure we probably will eventually, but they're doing alright for now.

"Well then, I guess we have to go to the grocery store," Tana says and glances at me.

Talk about a sucker punch. All I could imagine while she was in the hospital was having her back home, and now that she's here, it's bittersweet. I'm glad she's safe, I'm glad she's home, but I'm scared I'll never get her back. How can you mourn someone when they're right in front of you?

Clearing my throat, I say, "Well, load up. I guess we're going to get all the fixings for spaghetti."

Gemma squeals and Paisley looks a little lighter than she

has in a long time. Tana hangs back while the girls sprint to the truck to climb inside. She glances at me a little warily.

"I hope that's okay."

I want to take her hand and squeeze it to reassure her like I've done a thousand times before, but I know how physical contact makes her nervous. "Sure. We gotta eat it sometime. I appreciate you indulging them. I know it's hard on everyone."

Tana lifts a shoulder. "They seem like nice kids. And besides, I figure doing things they're used to might be a way to jog my memory."

I chew over that statement as we get loaded up in the car. The girls chatter excitedly in the backseat, and a quick glance in the rearview mirror shows them content for now. Tana buckles in quietly and clasps her hands tightly in her lap.

This must all be so strange for her. We're all essentially strangers, and she has to fit herself into a life that's supposed to be hers, yet she has no memory of. What a cluster.

"Is there anything else you need?"

Her eyes dart to mine. "What do you mean?"

"From the store. Anything you want to eat? Anything like toiletries or whatever?" I say the last awkwardly because even though we've been married for more than a decade, this isn't the same woman. We've been thrown into this forced intimacy without even knowing each other. Like an arranged marriage, for fuck's sake.

"I—I'm not sure. I hate sounding helpless, but I don't know anything. You basically have a third child." She chuckles nervously.

My heart squeezes in my chest. She can't quite meet my eyes, and her whole body is tense. I've got to remember to take it slow with her. Be careful with her.

"I know this is hard on you. I can't even imagine. But I hope you know I'm here for you, whatever you need. We'll go to the store, get stuff for supper, and see if there's anything else you need."

Tana shakes her head. "You don't have to do that."

"Of course I do," I say as though it's the easiest thing in the world. Because it is. She may not remember me, but she's my wife. I would do anything for her.

She sighs. "I may not know much, but I'm starting to learn that you are the most hardheaded man I've ever met."

At this, I crack a smile. "Have you met many men?"

Scowling, she says, "That's not the point. I keep trying to tell you that you don't have to take care of me, and you're not listening."

I glance at her pointedly as I pull to a stoplight. "I hear what you're saying. And, yeah, maybe I am hardheaded. But I vowed to take care of you, and that's exactly what I'll do. If that means giving you a safe place to stay while you figure things out, I'll do it. If it means taking you to and from doctor's appointments, I'll do it. And if it means things don't turn out quite the way I want them to, I'll deal with it. You let me worry about all that. You just worry about healing."

When she speaks, her voice is thick with emotion. "You don't even know me."

My hands clench the steering wheel. "I know you as well

as I know myself. And even if I didn't, it's the right thing to do."

She's quiet for a long time. We're nearly to the grocery store when she says, "I just don't wanna hurt you."

I glance in the rearview at the girls, who are now watching a movie on their respective tablets. They have headphones on, so they can't hear us talking. I turn to Tana and say, "You let me worry about that. I'm a big boy; I can handle it. In the meantime, I've been thinking about how to help you."

She raises her eyebrows. "More than you already are?"

"I mean with your memories."

She angles her body toward me. "Yeah? How are you going to help with that?"

"Well, I've known you most of your life. We share a lot of the same memories. Obviously, you can ask me if you have any questions, but I think it might help if you actually saw the things we were talking about."

"Do you mean like take me places?"

"Yeah, sort of. Take you to some of your favorite places, look through pictures, stuff like that."

"Don't you already have your plate full? You have two kids and your job. I can do some of the stuff on my own."

"Now who's being hardheaded?"

Tana rolls her eyes. "I have a feeling arguing with you could be a full-time job."

I pull into a parking lot spot at the grocery store and cut the engine. "Get used to it. That's probably the first thing you should know about me. It's something that you used to complain about quite frequently. Besides, you told me that acts of service is my love language. Doing things for other people is sort of how I live my life. It's why I became a paramedic. So it's only natural to me to want to help you."

When she starts to speak, I shake my head and say, "Just think about it."

The girls are unbuckling their seatbelts and throwing themselves out of the car. I help them and meet Tana at the front of the truck. Normally I would take her hand with Gemma to my right, and Paisley would grab Tana's free hand. But Paisley pauses awkwardly, so I take Paisley on my left and Gemma on the right. Tana doesn't seem to notice the moment of awkwardness.

"Come on, Paise. Let's see what we can get for dessert." I don't normally agree with sugar as a stopgap, but the girls have been through enough. Besides, cheesecake was Tana's favorite dessert ever. I wonder if it still is.

Time to put my theory to the test.

CHAPTER 6
TANA

"This is delicious." I savor the piece of cheesecake on my tongue, my eyes slipping closed.

"Yum," Gemma says. "Can I have another piece?" My eyes open to find Gemma winking owlishly at her father.

He laughs and gestures toward the cheesecake. "Fine, one more piece, but that's it. And I don't want any arguing about shower and bedtime."

Nodding enthusiastically, Gemma practically bounces in her seat as Alec serves her another piece.

"Me too?" Paisley asks.

Alec adds another piece to her plate, too. He turns to me almost out of reflex and gestures with the fork toward the cheesecake. "You want some more?"

I nod. "Thank you."

"You're welcome. I don't want any arguing about bedtime from you either."

I laugh, saying, "You won't get any arguments from me. I didn't sleep very well in the hospital, and I'm really looking forward to having my own room. Thank you again for letting me have the space."

"It's no trouble. It was yours anyway."

I frown at his words. "What do you mean it was mine?"

"The room used to be your office and craft room. It's where you spent a good chunk of your time. You should be comfortable there."

This must be where I ran the business he told me about. I checked out the social media platforms on the phone I was given while I was in the hospital, but it was immediately overwhelming. I don't know what I was expecting, but it wasn't the hundreds of thousands of followers across YouTube, TikTok, and Instagram. The sheer number of comments from people wondering where I was, speculating about what happened, and other wild things sent me spiraling. I can barely hold a conversation; how am I supposed to take up the mantle of super-influencer?

When I don't answer, he keeps rambling. "When the girls were little, you used to do things for fun. You'd make their outfits or their costumes or whatever. But when they got older and started going to school, you started making things for all of their friends and then the other kids in school. Eventually, you opened a shop online and started your own business."

I mull that around in my head as I finish the last few bites of cheesecake. Turns out I love spaghetti, and I would die for cheesecake. I can't imagine myself as a businesswoman. A person like that has to be highly motivated, organized, and driven. Is that me? I guess I'll have to find out.

"Bath time," Alec says firmly once the girls are finished.

As promised, they don't argue and go up to get their pajamas and take turns in the bath.

"I'll help you with that." I get up from my seat and start clearing the table. Alec is at the sink rinsing off the dishes and loading the dishwasher.

"I've got it."

"I thought you said you were going to help me with my memories. I'm pretty sure I've washed a dish or two in my lifetime. This could be helpful."

He huffs out a laugh. "Well, I'm not going to argue with you about it."

"Thank you."

We work together in a surprisingly comfortable silence. He puts away food and sets the dishes next to me on the counter. I rinse them off and load them in the dishwasher. He doesn't pester me with questions or inane chatter. And I'm grateful for the time to process the afternoon.

Shopping with Alec and the girls was an experience. The girls are lively, vivacious, and adorable. Gemma, with her boundless energy, practically bounced off the walls, and Paisley seemed to study everything with eyes much too mature for her age. They helped me pick out a new toothbrush, shampoo and conditioner, body wash, deodorant, and everything else I could need. I tried to protest, but Alec insisted, and I was tired of arguing with him. The overabundance of choice was overwhelming, to say the least. After a time, I let them pick out everything. How does one even choose a favorite scent? There are so many to pick from. I make a mental note to get something new every time I go to the store until I find something I like.

Then, we got the ingredients for spaghetti and meatballs. Alec insisted on cheesecake, and once he mentioned dessert, the girls wouldn't be swayed. I spent most of the time with my eyes darting back and forth, taking everything in.

Even though the girls are young, they know almost everything about making spaghetti. I almost thought ten-year-old Paisley could've done it on her own if I wasn't there. Under Alec's watchful eye, they helped me step by step, and by the end, I was surprised I didn't burn anything. The kitchen surely helped. It had everything from a little pasta water faucet to a gorgeous tub-like sink. It occurred to me as I was washing the dishes that I had probably picked everything in here out. It felt strange, like being in someone else's skin in someone else's house.

Alec works around me, wiping down the table, pre-packing the girls' lunches for school the next day, and sipping from a bottle of beer. I appreciate him going through the motions of a normal day and allowing me to be somewhat of an observer. It keeps the pressure off me. Even the girls were good about giving me space.

I have to wonder how long their patience with me will last. My thoughts begin to wander as I lose myself in my task. They can't always indulge my discomfort and can't always give me the space I'll need. Alec can't wait forever for his wife to come back, if she ever does. . .

But I also have nowhere to go. No idea what to do.

And his suggestion to bring back my memories seems as good a start as any. In the best-case scenario, the refresher works, and we go back to a relative normal. Worst-case scenario, I never get my memories back, and nothing has changed. In the meantime, it'll give me a chance to acclimate, heal, and figure out my next moves.

That doesn't mean I'm going to trust him right away. I'll let him try to bring my memories back—maybe I feel like I owe him that much—but I won't let myself trust him too much. If I do and shit goes sideways, I'm not sure I'll survive it.

CHAPTER 7
ALEC

"Thank you for helping," I say to Tana once the dishes are done, and the kitchen is clean. "But I don't want you to push it too much. The doctor said you should ease back into things."

Tana wipes her hands on a dishtowel and leans against the counter. Moonlight streams in from the window at her back, turning her hair into a golden halo. "Maybe we should set some ground rules."

I pull out a stool from the kitchen island and give her my full attention. "Shoot," I tell her.

"I don't want you to treat me like a damaged person." When I open my mouth to object, she holds up a hand. "Let me finish. Please."

Nodding, I gesture for her to continue. I'm gonna have to remember to give her space, let her speak her mind. So much of my professional life is spent taking charge, figuring out how to solve problems and fix things, that I'm finding it's all I want to do with Tana. Fix her. It's the worst feeling in the world to realize that maybe this is one thing I may not be able to fix.

"Thanks. Um, well, like I said, I don't want you to treat me like I'm damaged. I need you to be honest with me, even when I'm being a bitch." She pauses as though she's expecting me to object, but she gives me a half-smile when I don't. "I deserved that. Anyway, so rule number one is honesty. Without that, we have nothing."

"I agree. I'll be honest with you. In return, I want you to promise you won't hold anything back. If you're getting uncomfortable or need space, just tell me. I know the girls and I will have a lot of expectations from you. If it gets to be too much, you gotta let me know so we can let you breathe."

"Okay, we can make that rule two, and it goes both ways. If my being here is too hurtful for you or stressful for the girls, tell me so we can work something else out. I don't ever want to be a burden to any of you."

She has her arms crossed over her stomach in a protective gesture. I'd give anything to wrap my own around her and hold her close against me. I'd give anything to feel hers wrapped around me. I've missed her so fucking much, and it's killing me not being able to hold her, touch her.

"And don't say I'm not a burden," she warns before I can say exactly that. "We both know how hard this is on everyone. If it gets too hard, I'm giving you a free pass to tap out."

There won't be a free pass as far as I'm concerned. I'll do

whatever it takes to make this work and get my wife and the mother of my children back. But I know that would only upset her, so I say, "Same goes for you."

"Then I'll agree to these trips down memory lane." She shifts from foot to foot, and a vein hammers in her throat. "I mean, if you still want to."

"Of course, I want to. All I want is to help you."

Tana clears her throat. "Good, then whenever works for you."

I consider this for a minute. "Why don't we aim for Friday? That will give you a couple days to settle in, get your bearings. How does that sound?"

"Perfect." She hesitates, and I'm struck dumb when she smiles a little and the dimple in her cheek winks at me. It reminds me so much of our first kiss and the awkward goodbye at her door that I momentarily lose the ability to breathe. My heart thuds dully in my ears until she says, "Well, I'm going to get some sleep. Thank you again for everything today."

"You're welcome, Tana."

With another tremulous smile, she ducks her head and heads toward the spare room. My eyes follow her until the door closes behind her. I down the rest of my beer in one long gulp.

"Shh, you don't want to wake Mom up," I hear bright and early the next morning.

I lie awake in bed like I had most of the night and blink blearily at my ceiling, trying to wake the rest of the way up.

"Do you think she wants some breakfast? Maybe we should check." Gemma's whisper is more of a half-shout. I'm certain if Tana isn't awake already, she will be soon if the girls keep it up.

I peel myself from the bed with reluctance and slip a pair of shorts on. The girls are huddled at the entrance to the back hallway when I find them, contemplating whether or not to wake Tana up for breakfast. They lurch guiltily when they hear me clear my throat.

"What did I say about bothering her in the morning?" I ask as I move to start a cup of coffee and pull out the fixings for yogurt and fruit for the girls.

"See?" Paisley says smugly. "I told you we weren't supposed to wake her up."

Gemma pouts and digs into her breakfast as soon as I place it in front of her on the island, her disappointments soon forgotten.

"That's right. We need to let her settle in, and you both need to get to the bus stop for school. We're running a little late as it is."

They slurp down their yogurt without any major inter-ruptions and get their teeth brushed, lunches grabbed, and backpacks on just in time for the bus. A miracle. Mornings were never my thing. I'm more of a night owl, spending most of my evenings tinkering in the quiet solitude while Tana and the girls slept peacefully. She was the one who'd wake up before the sun to reply to emails or social media comments, work on orders, and have a full breakfast ready for everyone by the time we rolled out of bed.

I add that to the list of things I miss about her as I run through a checklist of what I need to do while the girls are at school. Run a load of dishes. Start some laundry. Order new school uniforms for both of them. Check the mail, pay bills. I'd be lying if a said I didn't realize exactly how much Tana took care of around the house until she wasn't there to do it anymore. I vowed that if she made it out of the hospital, I would never take her for granted again.

I'm finishing up on the computer and doing some mental calculations—we'll *just* scrape by this month, barely—when I hear the spare bathroom toilet flush I check my watch and absently note the time, nine a.m. Pushing to my feet from the little desk nook just off the kitchen, I pour a cup of coffee, hesitating over how to prepare it and decide to leave it black. Then I plate up eggs, avocado, and toast.

When she walks out, one hand lifted to rub at her eyes, my heart nearly leaps out of my chest. I gulp, my mouth going dry. She's dressed in a pair of my old gym shorts that are baggy at her hips and a tight little tank top with nothing underneath. It pulls tight at the softness of her belly and dips low over her generous breasts. I damn near swallow my tongue, but she doesn't seem to notice my reaction.

"Good morning," she says with a yawn and a delicate little sniff. "Something smells good."

Be cool. "Breakfast," I say and give myself a mental pat on the back.

Her eyes brighten, and she sits at the island in front of her plate. "This looks wonderful. Thank you. I'll have to learn how to make you breakfast, too."

I nod noncommittally and force myself to face away from her to clean up the dishes so I don't freak her out by staring. I can't believe I'd almost forgotten how fucking sexy she looks in the morning. All soft and sleep-rumpled.

She likes to linger over breakfast—her favorite meal of the day—catch up on chores around the house, and then take a shower and get ready for the day. It's torture sitting here and not reaching for her, pulling her back to the bedroom to make her dirty enough to need a shower.

My cock grows hard in my shorts just imagining it, so I busy myself with anything and everything in the kitchen while I rein in my thoughts. The last thing Tana needs right now is me salivating over her. "What do you have planned to do today?" I ask her once I get control of myself.

She takes a drink of the coffee—black because I wasn't certain how she'd take it now—and then winces. She sets it down while she adds hefty doses of cream and sugar. I focus on her cup as she brings it to her lips. This time it's not because her mouth, full and soft, parts and gives me a glimpse of her pretty pink tongue. No, it's because that's how she's always taken her coffee, too light and sweet to even taste like coffee anymore. I wonder if that's significant.

The doctor said matters of amnesia aren't an exact science. If you'd asked me before, I would have said a person is a sum of their experiences. Medically, if they don't have those experiences anymore, wouldn't it make them a different person?

I give myself a mental shake and refill my mug. As much as I'd like to have answers, Tana doesn't need me psychoanalyzing her every move. She has enough to deal with as it is without worrying more.

"I thought I might walk around town, see if I can't familiarize myself with everything."

My first reaction is to ask if she thinks that's wise, but I hold my tongue. If I were in her shoes, I'd want to do the same thing. I can't keep her under my watchful eye forever.

"That sounds like a good idea. You can use my bike if you want."

She brightens. "Are you sure?"

I retrieve the keys from a pegboard beside the garage door and set them on the counter next to her finished plate. "My only condition is that you keep your new phone on you, just in case you get lost or something."

"Of course," she says and gets to her feet. "I can't tha—"

"You don't have to keep thanking me, Tana."

She bounces on her toes. "Right. Well, I'm going to get ready. Don't feel like you have to wait around on me all day. I'll be fine, I promise, and I'll call you if I get into any trouble."

I give her a nod because what else can I do? I can't keep her in a protective bubble forever; she'll only grow to resent me. If I were in her shoes, I'd want the freedom to explore too.

But when she leaves an hour later, there's a sour feeling in my stomach.

I'd much rather have her in my line of sight where I can make certain nothing will ever happen to her again.

CHAPTER 8
TANA

Friday dawns, and I'm up with the sun. I've spent the past two days borrowing Alec's bicycle to cruise around Battleboro, hoping something about the town will jog my memory, but nothing does. It's like visiting a foreign country. Nothing about it is familiar.

It's disheartening, but what did I expect? To have an epiphany the moment I got on my own? Ridiculous.

Now it's time for Alec to take me to a place that's important to him and before-me. I was up half the night trying to imagine where it could be. Our first date? The place he proposed? Where we got married? The hospital where the girls were born?

You'd think if I were going to remember anything, it would be here, at home, where I spent most of my time with my family, but so far, nada. Zilch. My brain may as well be filled with tumbleweeds.

If I don't get out of bed right away, I'll spend the

morning moping, so I force myself to my feet and make the bed. That way, I'm not tempted to climb back in. Alec has made breakfast for the past three days, and when I find the kitchen empty, I get to work making him and the girls breakfast. It's the least I can do to repay them for being so kind and generous.

I don't change out of the soft and comfy pajama pants I found in the drawers, along with the Battleboro Fire & Rescue T-shirt, as I whip together cheese-topped scrambled eggs and thick sausage with fat juicy grapes. Paisley and Gemma arrive just as I'm plating everything up.

"Good morning," I say cheerfully, and they climb onto the seats at the island. It doesn't escape my notice that we gather in this room more than anywhere else.

"Mornin'," Paisley says with a wide yawn.

"Grapes!" Gemma cheers and stuffs her mouth full.

They sit in contented quiet and eat their breakfast. Alec joins at some point—shirtless and in a similar pair of pajama pants. I cover my look of surprise with a deep drink from my coffee mug. *Don't even go there, Tana.* But my inner warning doesn't stop me from sneaking a peek at a shirtless Alec.

He doesn't notice as he gets his own mug and pours a steaming cup. But I notice. I notice everything. His ab muscles—all eleven thousand of them—ripple then contract when he reaches up. I may not know a damn thing about myself, but I do know Alec Dorran is the sexiest man I've ever seen, and I can say that for a fact.

I manage not to drool much as Alec bundles the girls off to school. I've kept out of their way as they go about their daily routines. It's important to me to keep the girls' lives as normal as possible, and Alec seems to have everything well in hand for now. Gemma and Paisley wave goodbye as they get onto the bus, leaving Alec and me alone.

He turns to me—finally with a shirt on—and asks, "Well, are you ready for today?"

"Define ready?"

Alec gives me an easy smile. "Don't worry, we're going to start off easy. I thought we could go to the station so you could see where I work. Since I'll be there for the weekend, I figured maybe I'd give you a tour. Let you meet the guys."

I perk up. This feels fairly innocuous and low-pressure, which is probably why he chose it. Plus, fire trucks and ambulances. "Really? Could I ride in the ambulance?"

He rocks on his heels. "Sure, we could take a ride around the block. You sure that won't bother you? I know how much you hate hospitals at the moment."

I shake my head and say, "No, this sounds like fun. I'll go get ready."

I t makes me a little nervous to think of meeting the people Alec works with. I haven't done much interacting with anyone else yet, but I have to break the ice sometime. It may as well be now. Besides, I'm exceedingly curious about how Alec is with others. I want to see how other people view him and if it'll put my fears to rest or add to them.

After a shower, I agonize over what to wear and decide on

a pair of jeans and a bright red T-shirt. It's simple and comfortable. Besides, these people were the ones who responded to my accident. I doubt they really care what I'm wearing.

I find Alec in the living room surfing on his phone. "Ready to go?" he asks.

"As I'll ever be," I answer.

He looks up from his phone and visibly stills. All my muscles tense as he studies me. Oh, God, is he staring at my scars? I've tried to cover them up with my hair, but he doesn't say anything.

I follow him out to the truck, my nerves jangling. Maybe going to see his work isn't the best idea. There will be a lot of people there, people who know me, know him. *Get ahold of yourself, Tana.*

The station is a short drive away from our little suburb, and we arrive all too soon. Certainly not long enough for me to get control of my nerves. It's a small metal building with two roll-up doors on either side. One of them stands open with a fire truck facing out. Two guys are going through the compartments and marking things off clipboards. They look up when we pull to a stop.

The first is tall and lean with a swath of dark hair and intense eyes. I stiffen, waiting for some spark, reaction, or recognition, but nothing. Nada. No matter how many times it happens, it still surprises me. I really don't remember anything or anyone.

The second—who I don't recognize either—looks up as Alec comes around to help me down from the truck. He's in

Battleboro Fire & Rescue sweats and a T-shirt with the letters EMT over his left pec. He's taller than the first guy and broad across the chest. His sandy blonde hair is trimmed in a tight, almost severe crop. The way he carries himself is precise and exacting. I bet he's one of those guys who labels the food in his pantry and lines up his drinks in his fridge.

They straighten and move toward us. I immediately deduce the first guy is Alec's partner. His eyes light up in friendly greeting, and he moves to Alec to clap him around the back with a loud, slapping man hug.

The blonde in the back hangs back and observes instead of coming forward with the dark haired one. He nods in greeting when Alec says hello. I don't get an antagonistic vibe from him, more the strong silent type.

"Tana," says the dark-haired guy. "I'm Walker, Alec's partner."

I shake his hand, but he pulls me in for a hug. When we part, I babble. "I'm sorry I don't remember you, but you obviously know my name."

"Shit, we're just glad you're okay. It was a gnarly accident."

I don't know why it didn't occur to me that he would have been there but of course. I learned enough about the accident to know Alec was one of the responders to it. Since Walker is his partner, it makes sense he'd be there too.

I wince a little and say, "Yeah, so I've been told."

"Tana, this is Remington Davis, but we call him Remy."

Remy gives another nod in my direction. I was definitely right about the strong, silent type. "Hello," I say in as steady a voice as possible. He's the sort who doesn't have to say a word or do anything but can make you nervous from gravitas alone. I inch toward Alec without thinking. "Nice to meet you both. Again, I guess." I give a little nervous laugh.

"Everyone else inside?" Alec asks, and we move to a door on the right side of the building.

"Nah, Zeke and Jax are running a call right now, but they should be back soon."

The door opens to a nondescript hallway. There's another door off to the left, and Alec says to me, "That's Zeke's office. He's our captain."

I nod and stick to Alec like a shadow. It was different when I was in the hospital bed, thinking about getting out and figuring out everything I didn't know about my life. Now that I'm doing it, it feels overwhelming. Scary. I'm half-tempted to beg Alec to take me back to the house so I can hide under the covers in my bed and never come out. Even riding around town gave me distance from the people and things from before-me's life. This? Meeting them makes everything even more real.

Before I can get the words out, he's moving through another doorway to the right. Now we're in an open area that looks like a living room. Instead of the usual furniture, it's filled with a half-dozen recliners and a wall of walkie-talkie radios. To my immediate left is an open kitchen space with an island and four, yes, *four*, refrigerators. There are pieces of computer paper with 'A Shift,' 'B Shift,' and 'C Shift' written on them, which makes sense once I think about it. If they have a bunch of different people rotating in and out, they'd want a place to store their food for each shift so it's all in order and separated.

Walker throws himself in a recliner, and Remy disappears down a hallway to the right of the kitchen and living space. I glance that way curiously but follow Alec as he walks me through the little cubby area to the left of the kitchen, where there's a bank of computers softly humming.

"This is where we write all our reports," he says. There's an entire wall with laptops in protective cases and two desktop computers. He points to a door in the center. "That's Zeke's private bathroom and showers. This is the common space. Nothing too special about it, but we're pretty proud of our coffee bar." He and Walker share a significant look.

"Is there an inside joke about coffee I don't need to know?" I tease, trying to squash my own nerves.

Walker grins. "Well, it's just Alec was new here after the storm like I was, and when you saw that our old station had been demolished and we were living in old, busted temporary trailers, you raised a stink until we were finally given this new place complete with a coffee bar."

I glance between the two of them. "You're kidding. I did that?"

"You started it when you saw that the subfloors were rotting out from underneath us, and we were working double shifts." Walker sips from a mug of steaming coffee. "And we're very grateful still."

Swallowing hard, I try to give him a cheerful smile, but it feels forced. I don't feel like the kind of woman who could spearhead a campaign of that magnitude. No wonder Alec had been so distraught about losing before-me. Great mother, loving wife, concerned citizen. Was there anything about her that hadn't been perfect?

"Why don't I give you the rest of the tour?" Alec suggests.

"Sure." I give Walker a small awkward wave as Alec tugs me down the hallway where Remy disappeared.

Doors line either side, and Alec says, "These are our bunkrooms. We switch out with each shift, but we're lucky enough to have our own room."

I don't know what to say to that, so I just make an appropriate sound of approval. Alec opens the door to a room at the end of the hallway, and I'm immediately assailed by his scent. It's nothing fancy—a bed, a chair, a TV, and a good-sized closet. It's empty, and the bed is bare. The closet is split down the middle with labels on each half. Dorran is on the right.

"It's nice," I say. I imagine him sprawled out on the bed in only those sleep pants like he'd been this morning. He'd have one hand resting low on his stomach and the other under the pillow.

I jump when he starts talking again. "It's not much, but I figured I'd show it to you so you could get to know me a little more."

My face is flushed, but I hope he doesn't pay too much attention. It's only natural, I try to tell myself, and then push the image from my mind. "What do you do when you're not at work?"

Okay, maybe I am a bit curious. Who wouldn't I be? This is the man I was—am—married to. Part of me wants to know who he is and what drew me to him. I want to know the man before-me vowed to spend my life with. Maybe I owe it to him—to myself—and to the girls to be open-minded, give this at least a chance.

Alec points to the door, and I follow him back through the hallway. "We've got time. Why don't I show you?"

"Sure, why not?"

We wave goodbye to Walker, who raises a hand, then get back in the truck. "How long have you been here?" I ask.

"We moved here from Tallahassee four years ago after the storm because we wanted to be closer to my family. They also desperately needed EMTs and medics."

He drives the truck with an easy confidence, one hand on the wheel, the other propped on the window. It's a confidence I envy. I've only known Alec a short while, but it's been long enough to know that he's a man secure in himself, capable. A man who knows what he wants.

It hits me then that he must want me.

Then I remember we were in the middle of a conversation. "Do you like it here? I imagine it's different from Tallahassee."

He lifts a shoulder. "Not as much as you'd think other than Tallahassee has a hell of a lot more people. Besides, I think the pace here is much better, and we have a lot more room for the girls."

"Was I a good mom?" I blurt. I can't seem to wrap my head around the reality of it all. It seems to come naturally to Alec, like he was built to be a dad.

His gaze darts to me. "Of course you were," he says

without hesitation. "You *are* a wonderful mother, Tana. Don't ever doubt that."

Thankfully, we pull to a stop because I'm embarrassed about asking the question. It's not until we get out of the truck that I pay attention to our surroundings. It's some sort of park based on the tall, somewhat bare trees and playground off in the distance. It's scraped new like most of the landscape around Battleboro; the trees left standing are nearly naked, with just the slightest bit of regrowth on the limbs and downed trees everywhere. The fencing along the playground looks new, and so does some of the equipment.

To the right of the parking lot is a boat ramp, and the sound of trickling water fills my ears. What is it about running water that makes your muscles instantly loosen? I wonder if it's the same for everyone else when Alec takes my hand and helps me down the steep slope to the riverbank.

The river is about a football field wide and still high and dark green from the spring rain, I'm assuming. Cypress and oak trees line either side, and I imagine before the hurricane, it was a beautiful sight. A sign at the edge of the bank says, "Little Florida River."

"We spend a lot of time here," Alec says and tucks his hands into his pockets. "Fishing a lot of the time. Both of the girls learned how to swim here. We go tubing in the summer. My parent's place is just down a ways."

"It's beautiful here. Peaceful. I can see why you like it."

"It's also where we had our first kiss," he says, and my eyes fly to his.

I want to express the shock that crashes over my system,

but I can't find the words to speak, so a strangled sound comes out instead.

"I've debated how I'd handle this for a long time, and I didn't know for certain until now, seeing you here. This morning I thought it would be best to give you space to find your bearings, to heal and get acclimated." He moves closer, and my body freezes. "Now, seeing you here, remembering the first time you let me have your mouth, I realize that would be fucking stupid. I've loved you most of my life. I imagined spending the rest of ours together so often I can't picture a future without you. Like hell am I going to give you space to find a future without me in it."

"Alec—" My heart leaps into my throat.

He turns to me, his hand coming out of his pocket to thread through my hair. I can't move a muscle. I know the smart thing to do is to move away. To put back up the boundaries I've tried so hard to erect since I woke up in the hospital, but a voice inside my head tells me to wait. Just wait. See if there *is* something still inside me that cares for him as much as he obviously cared about before-me.

Which is why, when he uses that hand cupping my head to bring me forward, I don't resist. My hands fly to his chest, but only to ground myself against his solidity. Just one kiss. What could it hurt?

Oh.

His soft lips brush mine, and I instantly realize my mistake. Then my thoughts go quiet, and the sound of the river rushing by is all that fills my head. There is only the soft caress of his fingertips against my skin, the tender press of his mouth. A sigh shudders out of me, and I find my knees buckling. He takes my weight in stride, his arms around me to hold us both up.

I make a sound of need against his lips, and my eyes pop open. Pulling away, I try to remember all the reasons this was a bad idea. But all I can think about is wanting to do it again.

CHAPTER 9
ALEC

I don't know what I expected, kissing her. For her to magically recover her memory? Like I'm Prince Charming healing her with true love's kiss.

Of course, that doesn't happen.

I'm holding onto her because I'm almost certain if I let go, she'll lose her balance. But she's pulling away to look at me like she doesn't know me.

And she doesn't.

Another man would apologize for kissing her, and maybe I should. I just can't find it in myself to do it.

"I'll take you back home," I say instead.

She takes a moment to gather herself and takes a step back. "Alright," is all she says, her expression unreadable.

The ride back to the house is quiet, and I can't tell if she's pissed off or not. Before the accident, Tana wouldn't have hesitated to let me know when I fucked up. She would have smacked me on the arm, cursed like a sailor, then made me grovel until she felt I had atoned appropriately.

Now, though, I don't know how the fuck to handle this Tana. It's screwing with my head. She looks, smells, tastes, and feels like my wife. But is she really if she doesn't remember me or our life together?

I'd hoped kissing her would erase my doubts and fears, but ironically, all it did was make me even more confused.

"Alec," Tana says, and I glance over at her.

"Yeah?"

"Tell me about our first kiss. Was it like that?"

Pain sears through my chest. "Do you really want to know all that?"

"Yes."

I don't second guess her. Maybe part of me wants to talk about it. The grief I haven't had an outlet for spills from my lips.

"Well, we were in our early twenties. We'd spent all day on the water, dicking around with our friends. Goofin' off, tubin', drinkin'. We hung around the same group of people but had never gotten together. You were buzzed real good and couldn't stop laughing. I couldn't stop staring at you. The way your face lit up when you laughed. It made my chest hurt."

I'm not normally the sort of man who likes to talk about his feelings. My go-to is doing. Fixing. Figuring. But there's no amount of medical knowledge, physical strength, or clever problem solving that will bring my Tana back to me. The only thing I can give her is honesty. Memories. And so that's what I do.

"Everyone had mostly gone, and I was gonna be your ride back to your house because you'd had a little too much to drink."

"Really?"

"You were having fun. You just graduated from college. I was on leave with the military. It was summer. And you had on the sweetest red bikini."

She rolls her eyes. "Of course, that's what you remember."

I can't help my grin. "Hard to forget."

"Is that why you kissed me?"

I cut a glance at her. "Actually, you kissed me."

"You're kidding."

Shaking my head, I say, "Dead honest. I had just finished loading all our stuff into the truck when you cornered me against the door. You looked at me with such a serious look that I stopped laughing at whatever dumb shit the other guys were doing. You asked me why I hadn't kissed you already. I was stunned. I asked if you were serious. You said yes. That you'd been waiting all day for me to make a move, and when I didn't, you decided to do it yourself. That's why you had a couple drinks. To work up the nerve."

"What did you do?" Her eyes are all on me. I can't get the taste of her off my lips.

"I tried to tell you that we should wait until we hadn't been drinking. But you said you couldn't wait anymore. You moved closer to me until you were pressed up against me. I could barely breathe. I didn't generally go after friends. I didn't want to make it awkward if things went bad. And it often did back then, especially since I was new to my work and still in the military. A lot of women don't like that kind of lifestyle." I rub a hand through my hair. "Anyway, I tried to explain all this to you, but you weren't having any of it. You told me you'd been waiting to kiss me for weeks. That you didn't care what I did. And that you couldn't stand not knowing if the kiss would live up to everything you imagined because I was planning to deploy not long after. And I wouldn't be back for a long time."

She angles her body toward me. "And I still went for it? You didn't mind me being so aggressive?"

I feel my lips tip up in a half-smile at the memory. And then I remember she'll never have the same memory. A memory that's an earmark of our history together. It's gone for her. But it's still there for me. Feelings are still there for me. I roll my shoulders. "You told me later that you didn't want to live a life based on what-ifs or should-have-beens." Our eyes meet for a moment. "No, I didn't mind. I'd been gone for you for a long time."

Her eyes drift out the window. "It sounds weird to talk about myself like I'm a different person, but thank you. I should know these things. The person I was sounds fun. And daring."

"You still are. Give yourself a break. You only just got out of the hospital. You're doing so much better than you were even a few weeks ago."

She sighs heavily and changes the subject. "What happened next?"

I don't press her. "I tried to tell you I didn't want to hurt you. But you told me to shut up and kiss you."

That startles a laugh out of her. "What? Really?"

"Not at all. Then you wrapped your hands around my shoulders, pushed up on your toes, and laid one on me. Other than the day we got married, it was the best kiss of my life."

She goes quiet for a while, but I don't push her. Frankly, I'm glad she's asking questions. Gives me time to process both the memories and the fact that I kissed her. It was probably a bad idea, but I couldn't not kiss her.

"I wish I could remember," she says, breaking through my thoughts.

She's not looking at me, but I can hear the sorrow in her voice. I hate that I caused it. "I wish you could too. But it's not your fault."

"I know. What did you do after I kissed you?"

I pull into the driveway at the house and turn to look at her. "Isn't it obvious?"

She unbuckles slowly and gives me a confused look.

Grinning, I say, "Oh, well, I kissed you back. And I was such a great kisser you convinced me to marry you."

She shakes her head, soft caramel blonde curls tumbling over her shoulders, and gets out of the truck. I join her as we walk to the front door. "I was due to deploy two months after that, and we spent nearly every moment together. I kept trying to reason with you, but you said it felt right. You told me that our souls recognized each other." I smile as I unlock the door, remembering how serious she'd been when she said it. "I'm not the sentimental type of guy, but I fell for it, and you, hard. So a week before I was due to deploy, I asked you to marry me. Without hesitating, you said yes. We had a quick courthouse wedding, and you had my ring on your finger by the time I flew out."

We move into the kitchen, where I fix leftovers for lunch. Eating in silence for a while, I catch Tana glancing at the ring on my finger. Hers had to be cut off after the accident. I saved the pieces, but there's no repairing it, so it's in the jewelry box on our dresser, a grim reminder.

"Why did you ask me to marry you after two months?"

I wipe my mouth with a napkin and study my hands. "It didn't feel like two months to me, to be honest. It felt a lot longer. All I knew was that when I faced deploying without you in my life, I couldn't leave without knowing you were mine. Permanently, legally, and everywhere I could have you. Maybe a little bit of your crazy rubbed off on me." I huff out a laugh.

"Doesn't sound any crazier than the situation we're currently in." When I look up at her, she giggles a little. Some of the tension in my chest releases. If I hadn't already kissed her, that little giggle would've made me kiss her for sure. I missed hearing it.

"I guess you're right about that. OK, I've got to get the girls from school and take them to my mother's house. Are you going to be okay here by yourself for a while? You'll have the rest of the weekend to yourself too. My mom will check on you to make sure you don't need anything. I figured you'd probably enjoy the freedom."

"Thank you. I appreciate that, but I think I'm OK. I'm planning to spend as much time as possible outside. After being cooped up in the hospital, all I can think about is being outside."

"That sounds like a plan to me. I'm going to leave you my card, so if you need anything just use it. The pin number is 4382."

She winces, and her shoulders tense up a little. I know she hates me taking care of her, but I don't know any other way to be. "Thank you," she says. I'm grateful she doesn't argue.

I hesitate before turning to go. I don't like leaving her alone. She's still bruised up and sore, and all I wanna do is hold her. I'm pretty sure if I started, I wouldn't be able to let go. It was a miracle I stopped kissing her in the first place.

Giving myself a little shake, I grab my wallet and keys. I need a mental buzzer every time I slip back into thinking things are like they used to be. They probably won't ever be. I need to remember that for all of our sakes.

When I can't drag it out any longer, I leave her with a wave. Mom promised to check in or do a little drive-by so I don't worry too much. When I get in the truck and drive away, there's a weight on my chest like I'm wearing fifty pounds of gear. It's harder than I thought to leave. Much harder than it was leaving her in the hospital. At least then, I knew she was being watched over twenty-four seven. At least then, I was selfishly sure she couldn't run away if she wanted.

I think about that on the way to the school to pick up the girls, through our goodbyes at my mom's, and on the drive to the station. Because she could now. She could leave if she wanted. If this is too hard, or if she realizes she doesn't love me or wants to have the girls. She could leave. And I couldn't blame her. The memories, feelings, and promises she made before the accident are gone. It's only whatever obligation and sense of morality she has inside her that keeps her with us. All of that could change in an instant.

And that scares the ever-living shit out of me.

CHAPTER 10
TANA

Later that day, I'm surprised to find myself missing Alec.

Which doesn't make sense. I barely know him. What's there to miss? Sure, he visited me every day in the hospital. Aside from the healthcare workers, he was my only other touchstone to my new life. It's probably just familiarity. Or what little familiarity we have.

It's probably because this is the first time I've had any real alone time since I woke up in the hospital. If he wasn't there visiting, nurses and doctors or specialists were coming in and out. There was just always someone around. Maybe I found comfort in the background noise of the hospital and staff and all the sounds around me. It reminded me I wasn't alone. Because now that there's no one else here, I'm alone with my thoughts. It's quiet, and there's only me.

True, Alec is a stranger, but so am I. There's a huge blank

spot where the old Tana used to be. And like the doctors have been telling me, I have to get to know the me I am now.

Before I give Alec or the girls answers or figure anything else out, I have to start there.

Talking to Alec helps. It gives me a glimpse into the life that I used to have. But I also want to figure some of those things out on my own.

This is the perfect time to do that. After he left, I wandered around like a lost kitten. I went from room to room just looking at things. I was mostly drawn to the girls' rooms. I didn't invade their space or go through any of their things. I just stood in the doorway and looked around, pretty much like a creep, but I didn't think they'd mind. Well, Paisley might've minded, so I didn't stay too long by her room. Gemma probably would have invited me in to play. It's incredible that I already have such a sense of them after such a short time. I wonder if that's some sort of maternal intuition coming out.

I did the same thing with the rest of the rooms in the house. Alec told me to make myself at home. He said nothing was off-limits. But I still felt weird going into his— our—bedroom. I don't think I'll ever get over how strange it is to know this house, this place and these things, belong to me yet feel so distant from all of it.

That sensation couldn't be more prevalent than when I open Alec's bedroom door and am bombarded with a variety of scents. The first is something floral, feminine. It must be my perfume. I think of Alec sleeping here, smelling my perfume, and being alone. A wave of empathy crashes over me. I wish this didn't have to be so hard on him.

There's nothing I can do about that. I feel I owe it to him and the girls—for caring for me—to learn more about the woman I used to be, so I head straight for the closet. I feel like seeing *her* clothes. And I have to think about before-me as *her* because she feels so separate. Seeing *her* clothes may help get a glimpse inside *her* head.

It's a generous walk-in closet. Alec's clothes and uniforms are to the right, and mine pretty much take up seventy-five percent of what remains. I guess in that aspect, we were pretty stereotypical. Even though I came into the closet to look at *her* clothes, I'm drawn to his instead.

I might as well get to know him as well. I don't think he'll mind. Hanging in neat lines on his side are several uniform T-shirts, tactical-looking pants, and other basic T-shirts, most of which look like they need to be thrown out because they're covered in grease stains, and God knows what else. There are a couple long-sleeved, button-down shirts that look dressier and then hoodies and jackets. But I don't see any regular, non-work pants. I know it's Florida, but it gets cold sometimes. Does he have some sort of grudge against pants?

The thought makes me smile because, of course, he would. I imagine if he's not at work, he's outside or playing with the girls. His style leans more toward efficient comfort. Which pretty much describes him, to my mind. But I can't help but think he would look great in a pair of somewhat fitted blue jeans. I may not remember him, but I know there's something about a man in tight jeans. My mouth waters at the thought of him in them, and I clear my throat even though there's no one around. I force myself to move from his side of the closet to what used to be mine. I've got to stop thinking of him like that, but thoughts of him have assaulted me ever since that kiss.

Stop thinking about it, Tana.

Does a woman even need this many clothes? As I rifle through them, my eyebrows move higher toward my hairline. There are dozens of blouses, skirts, pants, and dresses. Certainly, too many for one person to wear. I could pick one thing each day and still have more left at the end of the year. Before–me must have liked her clothes. Since the total of my wardrobe for the past month has been yoga pants or a hospital gown, all the fancy fabrics and indulgently flamboyant heels are overwhelming. Foreign. I've seen her Instagram, and while *she* was gorgeous, I just can't picture her influencer-chic style meshing with Alec's rugged simplicity. He must have really loved her.

Right now, I think I'd just be happy to dress more like Alec. Simple. Maybe a pair of shorts and a T-shirt. But I decide to try on some of the clothes anyway to see if I'm wrong. First, a summer sundress. It's beautiful, but I don't know. The dress fits me like a second skin, following my curves and accentuating my positive attributes while camouflaging my insecurities. I had to hand it to *her*; she had excellent taste. I feel like I'm playing dress-up in someone else's clothes.

I guess I sort of am.

I go through all the clothes and decide on a simple pair of jeans and a fitted T-shirt. Low-key, that's the new and improved Tana Dorran. She likes spaghetti and cheesecake and prefers shorts and a T-shirt to fancy dresses. There. At least I'm getting to know after-me. It's about damn time.

I spy a box with my name on it, but I don't want to invade Alec's privacy anymore, so I leave the bedroom and go downstairs to relax with some TV. I don't recognize any of the shows I see. There are dozens of apps to choose from, and I settle on some sort of crime show. After six episodes, dark has fallen, and I realize most of the evening has passed me by. Well, screw it. At least I learned something else about after-me. I like true crime. Now that I've been through my own horror story, it helps to see some of them tied up neatly with a bow. It was comforting that most of them were solved at the end of a half-hour. I wish my own problems could be solved as easily as those on TV.

I contemplate what to make for dinner when I hear a knock at the door. Thinking it may be Tracy, who Alec said might stop by, I cross to it shouting, "Just a second," before I look through the peephole and see a scruffy man I don't recognize. I shift from foot to foot as I consider what to say. The man gives an impatient huff and bangs his fist on the door again when I don't open it immediately. *Thump thump thump*. Dammit, I shouldn't have said anything.

My heart slams into my chest. It doesn't seem like this is a friendly visit from a neighbor. The scowl on his face makes deep grooves in his cheeks. His eyes are hazy red and unfocused. I imagine if there wasn't a door between us, the scent of alcohol would be noxious and overwhelming.

Nope. No way in hell I'm opening that door. Probably some guy who had too much fun on his Friday night and is looking for trouble.

Well, I've had enough trouble for a lifetime. I don't need any more.

"Open the door!" he shouts. Like that'll happen. What kind of delusional psycho thinks that would actually get someone to open the door? "Open the door, bitch. I heard you and know you're there."

Lovely. I throw the bolt and hook the security chain for good measure. He's still banging away, so he doesn't hear me. While he's distracted and hollering at the front door, I preemptively lock the back door, too. I give a passing thought to calling Alec, but he's busy at work. If worse comes to worst, I'll call the cops. For now, I barricade myself in the closet in my room and wait until it's quiet.

Thankfully, the drunk gives up after a couple more minutes of hollering. I come out of the closet and peer through the peephole, but the front porch is empty. What a freak show.

What I really want is a beer—do I even like beer?—but I don't find any in the fridge, so I settle for a glass of ice-cold sweet tea and bring it with me to the shower. The heat feels amazing. I swear the water never got quite warm enough at the hospital. I stay under the spray until the ice in my tea melts. I'm putting on a robe and thinking about vegging on the couch with more episodes of my latest true crime obsession when I hear another knock at the door.

Oh god, not again. This guy really needs to lay off the booze.

I peer through the peephole and find not the drunk but a woman on the other side. Relieved, I open the door and only remember I'm in a robe at the last second. "Yes?" I ask.

She's about my age with soft brown hair and thick-rimmed glasses. "Hey, Tana. I'm sorry to come over so late."

Squinting at her, I tug at the lapels of my robe. "That's okay. Um, I'm sorry, but what's your name?" I give her a sympathetic smile.

The woman smacks her forehead. "*Duh*, I'm sorry. I'm Angela, your next-door neighbor. I heard all the yelling and thought I'd check on you. I think my dad's been drinking again. I wanted to apologize if he scared you."

Relieved to have an explanation, my shoulders relax. "That was your dad?"

Angela leans against the doorjamb, sighs, and swipes some hair away from her glasses. She radiates the harried kind of anxiety I remember feeling after waking up in the hospital. "Yeah, Leon. He's had a rough week at work. You know how it goes." She lifts a shoulder.

"Thank you for letting me know."

Angela replies, pushing away from the door, "We're next door if you need anything. I'll keep a muzzle on Dad next time he gets into the beer cooler."

I laugh awkwardly and wave at her as she crosses the yard to a brick house on my left. The yard needs a serious trim, and there are two broken-down cars in the driveway. But who am I to judge? I can't even remember my own name sometimes. Closing the door, I push the interaction from my mind. I won't let one weird guy ruin my first free weekend.

I'm going to spend tonight binging more crime shows, and then tomorrow, I'm going to find an empty hiking trail to explore.

Of course, the true crime peeps on the show would probably tell me not to go hiking alone but screw that. I'll pack a can of hairspray or something for protection.

By the time I fall asleep a couple hours later, like so many other things, the whole interaction is forgotten.

CHAPTER 11
ALEC

The weekend without her is torture.

It drags on until I'm snapping at all the other guys, and I'm pretty sure they're scheming to tie me to the top of the ambulance by the time my shift is over.

Finally, Walker snaps. "Dude, if you don't sit down and stop pacing, I'm going to deck you."

I clean the kitchen for the second time. "Please. If it was Avery, you'd be doing the same thing."

He swings an arm over the back of the recliner he's sprawled in. "I'm not saying I wouldn't be going insane at leaving my woman alone. Hell, I moved back to Battleboro for Avery because I couldn't stand a few days without her. So, I understand. But that doesn't mean it isn't balls-out annoying."

"Just wish I didn't have to leave her so soon. You've seen how she is." Even the thought of her being by herself has me wanting to crawl out of my skin.

"How's she handling everything?" Walker asks with a tinge of amusement at my obvious discomfort.

I get a rag and start wiping down the already clean counters. "I don't know, man. I used to be able to read her. Now it's like she's written with a different code. I don't know a damn thing about her now."

Remy pushes back from the table and goes to the water machine to refill his cup. "Why don't you just call her?"

This coming from him is somewhat out of character. As far as I know, Remy doesn't date. In fact, there's been speculation around the station that he's either celibate or asexual. Not that I'm judging. Clearly, relationships are hard work. Even so, I wouldn't trade my relationship—with all its complications—with Tana for the world.

Finished scrubbing the counters, I put the clean dishes away. "I would, but I'm trying to give her some space. I can't do that if I'm bugging her every half hour."

Remy sips contemplated leave from his class. "I would just call her."

Maybe I should. But I get off shift in a few hours. If something was wrong, she would call me. Right?

The final few hours of my shift drag on. I prefer to stay busy as it keeps my mind off of things. In that respect, going back to work is a relief. Running calls and the monotony of paperwork help distract me from whatever Tana might be doing at home. Or how the girls are feeling. Or what the future is going to look like. Of course, this would be the one day we don't get any calls. Seriously. I would kill for a fucking heart attack or overdose. Normally I use the free time to catch up on coursework or finish reports, but all I can do is think about Tana.

My brain keeps wrestling with itself, trying to figure out a way to make everything work for everyone. But in this instance, there just aren't any easy answers. Only hard ones and more questions.

Finally, I get off work and head straight home. Mom is supposed to bring the girls over in time for dinner, which works as it'll give me some time to see how Tana is feeling.

As I turn into the driveway, my eyes cross over to the broken down cars at the house next door. I scowl, shoving down the surge of emotion at the sight and force my thoughts back to seeing Tana. I double-time my steps as I move to the door. I push it open, expecting to see Tana right away but am surprised to find the living room empty, the TV still blaring some true crime show, and loud music coming from the backyard. My brows pull together. My wife has never been the true crime sort. She always found that sort of thing too depressing. *The Kardashians* or *Real Housewives* was more her speed. And since when does she listen to country?

I call out her name, but she probably can't hear me over the music. My heart is galloping at the prospect of seeing her like it hasn't done in years. Don't get me wrong, I love my wife, but I haven't felt so excited at the thought of seeing her since we first started dating. There's an ease when you've been with a person for over a decade like we have. I'm not complaining about it. The only drama I like in my life is when I deal with emergencies at work. After Tana's accident, even that has lost a bit of his allure. But I have to admit I am enjoying feeling like we get to do a little of the dating dance again.

It's both a rediscovery of her. . . and of how we work together. If we still will. I'm looking forward to the challenge of proving I'm the only one for her. . . now and forever.

If this were the Tana before her accident, she'd be in the attic retrieving all of her supplies to get started on her latest project or business idea. If she wasn't doing that, she'd be coming back from a shopping trip, loaded down with dozens of bags.

But no.

I find her at the source of the music in the backyard, up to her elbows in the dirt, with the most adorable streak of grime on her cheeks. Did she forget to turn off the TV? The doctor said things like that would happen occasionally. I worry about whether she's forgetting other things until I realize she's wearing tight as hell cut-off jean shorts, her thighs lush and thick spread a little to compensate for her off-center gravity. And I am suddenly viciously reminded of them wrapped around my head. My mouth goes dry.

I ache with wanting her.

I always have, and I always will.

"What you doing there?" My voice comes out a little gruff.

She doesn't react. In fact, she digs another hole with a spade and flops a purple pansy down in the fresh hole. "Tana?"

She still doesn't seem to hear me over the sounds of the music and her singing along. And then her hips begin to do a little wiggle. *Goddamn.*

She asked me once before if I were an ass or tits man. I told her I was her man. But watching her shimmy and wiggle, I identify as an ass man. Ass, all the way. The way I would worship her if I could, she wouldn't be able to walk for a week. I'd show her exactly how much I missed her. Exactly how grateful I am that she's with me in any capacity, with any complications. I'd have it all. I want it all. I want her any way I can take her because there is no one else for me.

My cock grows painfully hard in my uniform pants. Blood pulses thick and hot, playing a wild tattoo in my veins. I have to get a hold of myself, but I can't seem to tear my eyes away from her ass. My knees buckle, and I fall into a garden chair and watch her plant flowers along the flowerbeds around our patio.

I can't seem to take my eyes off her. For the first time since the accident, she seems unburdened. And here I thought I'd come home and find her wallowing or frightened and hiding. Though I shouldn't be surprised she's doing the opposite. She's always been a fighter. In fact, of the two of us, I'd say she's the stronger one a thousand times over. I guess some things haven't changed.

I freeze when she shifts back on her heels and gets to her feet. Her knees are covered with dirt, and her gloved hands are caked in mud. Her face is sweaty and flushed, and her hair is coming free of the ponytail at her nape, but she has never looked more beautiful. Her face is still a halo of bruises underneath the pink flush from the sun, but she looks healthier than she has in a while. Vital. At least that's a relief.

Before she woke up in the hospital, I thought I was going to lose her. I imagined a thousand scenarios where her condition could suddenly destabilize, and she'd slip away from me. Seeing her alive and well and so goddamn beautiful it makes my chest hurt is a relief I can't quantify. The amnesia almost doesn't even matter anymore. She's here. She's *mine*. I just have to help her see it.

Tana jerks a little when she notices me sitting there. Turning down the music, she says, "Oh my God! You scared me. How long have you been sitting there?"

"Not long. Just got home." I nod to the flowers. "What are you doing here?"

She rubs a hand along her forehead, smearing more dirt and making me smile. "Well, I got bored hanging around the house. And I noticed the backyard looked a little sad, so I cut the grass and started weeding. Then it looked so bare I thought it needed flowers. I hope you don't mind. You said I could use your card, and I figured the girls would like it. I can pay you back if—"

I cut her off with a wave of my hand. "Don't be silly. I think it looks great. And you're right. Neither one of us had much of a green thumb in the past. So our yard suffered, and houseplants cowered in our presence."

She shifts from foot to foot and chews on her lip. And now all I can think of is sucking it into my mouth and biting down. "I guess I just like being outside, you know? Being cooped up room was driving me crazy."

I shift in the seat, trying to form coherent thoughts. "Oh, I understand. I'm glad you found something to keep busy with. How was your weekend otherwise?"

She nods and clears her throat, taking off her gardening gloves. "It was good. I rested a lot and watched a lot of TV. But otherwise, I didn't do too much. What about you? How was work?"

She takes a seat in the open lounge chair next to me, and I can't take my eyes off her bare legs. She's reclining, so she doesn't notice, thank God. "It was boring as hell. We only had two calls the whole shift."

She cracks open one eye, and I tear my gaze away from her legs before she catches me ogling. "And that's a bad thing?"

"Just makes for a very long, boring shift, that's all."

"What's a normal shift for you look like?" she asks.

Grateful for the distraction, I detail the long hours, monotonous paperwork, and occasional trauma I encounter on a typical shift. She listens with interest, her eyes on me, and it jars me to realize I have her full attention. Before, her thoughts would have wandered off, or her phone would have gone off with some crisis or another. I feel a little guilty to realize this version of my wife is different—and I like it.

Thankfully when I push to my feet a short while later, my erection is gone. "I'm gonna get a shower and make dinner for when the girls come home. Give me a shout if you need anything."

She nods and gets to her feet to clean up the empty pots. "I'll take one after you."

Oh shit. Now my imagination really goes wild. I nod awkwardly and leave before I do something stupid like tackle her to the ground and rip those little shorts off her legs to bury my face between her thighs.

"We should get a pool!" Gemma exclaims after she takes a long drink of milk.

I lift a brow at her. "A pool, huh?"

"Yeah," she explains. "Elizabeth and Maria from school both have one. It's going to be summer soon. We should get a pool."

"You don't even know how to swim," Paisley says with a tone of wry superiority that only an older sibling.

It doesn't seem to faze Gemma, who is used to her sister's attitude. "Then it will be the best time to learn. Mom can teach me."

"She could if you weren't scared to swim," Paisley says and rolls her eyes.

"So? Maybe if we get a pool, I won't be scared." Gemma juts out her lower lip.

"Yeah, right," Paisley retorts.

"All right, girls," I interject before it can turn into a screaming match. "I don't know about buying a pool, but I'll make sure we go swimming a lot this summer."

A glance at Tana, who has been quiet. I don't glean much from her expression other than curiosity. Like an observer at the zoo who's never encountered exotic creatures before. *Will I ever get used to this? Will it ever get easier?* I don't know.

I wanna dig my fingers in my face and shotgun about twenty beers. I keep waffling between protecting the girls and risking everything on this woman. Frankly, I'm getting sick of my own fucking thoughts.

I shove up from the table and get the girls' empty dishes. "Bath time. Paisley, you're first this time. No arguing."

She flips her hair at her sister and prances off. Gemma is naturally unfazed and studies me with a calculating eye. "Can I have more ice cream?" This girl. She will never fail to make me smile no matter what is going on.

I ruffle her hair. "Good try, squirt, but you've had enough for today. Go watch cartoons until your sister's done in the shower, and then it's your turn."

She shrugs her shoulders as though to say at least I tried and goes to the living room, where I hear the tinny sound of *My Little Pony* starting up. Wordlessly Tana helps me clear the rest of the dishes from the table and pack away the leftovers into Tupperware.

As we move around the kitchen cleaning up dishes and packing away food, all I can think of is her legs in those damn shorts. I'm hyperaware of her movements around me, sensitized to the max at being near her.

"You're so good with them," Tana says softly as she carefully stacks glasses in the dishwasher.

"They're going to make my hair turn gray before I'm forty-five."

Tana giggles, making me smile. "I guess you are outnumbered here, aren't you?"

"I've gotten used to being a girl dad. I think I wear it kind of well. Besides, I love being surrounded by my girls."

There's a contemplative pause, and then she says, "Did you want to have more children?"

My head snaps in her direction. When I can find my breath again, I say, "What?" is the only thing my tongue can spit out.

"I'm just curious. You never wanted to try for a boy?"

"It never mattered to me what we had. Girl or boy. You had rough pregnancies, and Gemma's birth was really hard on you. What I cared more about was that you were safe and healthy. So no, I don't think I want to have more children."

"It's strange to know that they came from me and yet not know them," she admits, the vulnerability stark on her face.

I take my time washing the next plate. I don't wanna say the wrong thing, not when she's opening up to me like this. The old Tana was so self-sufficient and self-assured that I didn't often have to be a shoulder for her like this. This new side of her is. . . Honestly, more attractive than I thought it would be. I always admired her strength and leaned on it more than once. But seeing her like this is new and makes my overprotective drive crank up to new levels.

"I don't know what to say other than I understand how hard this must be for you. You aren't alone in all of this. We have to lean on each other. You can lean on me, Tana. It doesn't matter how heavy the burden is. I'll carry it for you."

She tilts her head to the side and studies me. "Is that how it was for you—I mean us. . . before?"

"You mean trusting each other to share the hard stuff?" I ask.

Tana nods emphatically. "Yeah, how do you trust someone else to take care of you? To not drop the ball when it's important?"

I'm not the best with words. I do better with actions, but I don't want to mess this up or have her close up on me, so I try my best for the right thing to say. "I guess it takes time and the willingness to be hurt. A leap of faith. I don't expect that from you right away. All I'm asking for right now is just that. . . time."

"Well, we've got plenty of that, considering I have no life to speak of at the moment." She changes the subject. "How are you handling everything?"

I gave her a half-smile. "It's funny. The guys asked me that about you this morning. I'm doing as well as I can be."

"Do you mind if I keep asking you questions? I'm just curious about you and the girls and everything. I do want to get to know you. And them. I want to know the person I used to be. Maybe it'll help me figure out who I'm supposed to be now."

"Of course you can ask questions. I'm an open book. Ask me whatever you want."

"You may regret that in the future." She softens the tease with a genuine smile.

CHAPTER 12
TANA

I have to give it to him. He's answering every question with honesty and kindness. Even the sensitive ones. In the hour since the girls have gone to bed, we've talked about almost everything.

"Did you always want to be a first responder?"

Alec takes a sip of his beer and stretches his neck from side to side. "No. I toyed with a lot of career paths after I got out of the military. This one seemed to check all the boxes. I liked the idea of serving my community. Some people don't really like the emergency care, but I find it fascinating. I like the challenge."

Maybe that's why he's taken everything that's happened in stride. He's used to these kinds of situations. Probably not when they occur to someone he loves, but he's remained steadfast. That I learned quickly. He didn't hesitate to step up in any way possible when he realized I had amnesia. He took time off work to see me and take me to every appointment when I needed physical therapy after the accident.

Maybe that's how a husband is supposed to treat his wife, but it still surprises me. Am I the kind of person who could do that for someone else? Be that selfless? I don't know. That's the plain truth.

I just don't know.

"What about me? What did I want to do?"

He picks at the label on the beer bottle. "For the most part, you were content to stay home with the girls. At least until they got older. Then you got restless. You liked to fill your time with activities and trips, and you hated to be bored. What started as a hobby making things for the girls in your spare time just sort of evolved into a business and then exploded from there. We were both in awe of your success at first. But I shouldn't have been surprised. You often went after things and didn't stop until you succeeded. Kind of like how you went after me." I give her a cheeky smile.

"And you liked that?" I can't help asking. I'm curious. The more I learn about him, the more intrigued I become. This man would do so much for someone who doesn't even remember him or was even remotely nice to him at first. His patience and gentleness with the girls. His work.

It doesn't hurt that the more I'm around him, the more I actively have to try *not* to touch him. When he left in his uniform the other day, I nearly swallowed my own tongue. I imagined him hauling around a big hose, all sweaty and. . . heroic. Then I almost walked straight into a door.

"It was hard not to. You sort of broke down all my

barriers until I gave in." He smiles a little at this, and I realize the burning sensation I feel in my chest whenever he talks about before-me is jealousy.

I frown inwardly at myself. That's so ridiculous. How can I be jealous of myself?

"What if I'm nothing like that anymore?" I blurt out the question and feel a stabbing sense of insecurity. As much as I want to be on my own, I've grown to like Alec. . . maybe even care for him. Hard not to after he was so stubborn about seeing me every day in the hospital and then offering me a place to stay even when I wasn't so nice about it.

"What do you mean?" His tone is gentle and soft. A person could confess everything to a man with a voice like that.

"What if I'm not that girl anymore? Those memories, everything I lost. That's what makes a person. What if, without those memories, I'm not the same woman you married? What do we do then?"

He's quiet for a long time. Long enough that my heart beats a little faster. My hands are sweaty on my own beer bottle, but I resist the urge to wipe them on my thighs.

"I wish I had those answers for you, sweet pea. I wish I knew for certain how this will all end. The only thing I know and can control are my own actions. And since you're asking, I'll be honest with you."

Oh shit. I should've kept my mouth shut. Do I really want to know what he's going to say? Yes, I decide as he meets my eyes, ensnaring me with his powerful gaze.

"When I made those vows to you, to love, honor, and

cherish you, in sickness and in health, I meant them. You're still the woman I married. And I'm going to love, honor, and cherish you for as long as I have you. Now, if you decide being married to me isn't what you want any more, I'll respect that. Not happily and not without a fight, but I will respect whatever you feel you need."

"Without a fight?" What does that mean?

He reaches across the distance between us to sift his hand through my hair, sending shivers down my body. If that's what happens with just one touch, what would happen if he does more? I swallow hard as he begins to speak.

"I mean, I'll do whatever it takes. It's just how I'm wired. I couldn't save you from the accident. I can't give you back your memories. But I can honor my vows. I can be the man who promised you everything. Always. Not just because I'm obligated to you. But because I want to. For you."

I force myself to think through the instant searing hot lust. "You mean for *her*. The woman I used to be?"

His thumb traces my cheekbone, and I fight the urge to let my eyes flutter closed. "For her. And for you. The woman you are now. Marriage isn't a fleeting thing, Tana. We've both changed in the years we've been married. You aren't the same girl who kissed me by the river. And I'm not the same reckless guy who joined the Army. Marriage isn't just about loving each other at the moment. It's about forever. It's about the ups and downs and learning and growing with the person you want by your side. It's an investment. And a gamble. And I'll tell you now, no matter what happens, I will always gamble on you."

My breath evacuates my lungs. I don't know what to say. I mean, what can you say to that? I settle on, "Wow," and wonder if he's scrambled my ability to make coherent conversation or if it's the brain damage.

"What about you?" he asks.

I blink rapidly, trying to reign in my thoughts. "What about me?"

"What will you do if you never get your memories back? If you decide you don't want to stay here with us?"

"That's the question, isn't it? I have no idea. How can I decide on a future when I don't even know myself?"

"Luckily, neither of us has to do too much deciding tonight. We can take it easy while you get adjusted."

"You call that kiss from the other day taking it easy?" I say before I can think twice about it. I wonder if one of my post-accident symptoms is speaking without thinking because I can't seem to control the words coming out of my mouth where he's concerned.

I wasn't going to mention the kiss at all. In fact, I gave myself a firm talking-to about it all weekend. But the words are out there now, and I can't take them back.

"Considering what I still want to do to you, yes."

Oh my God, it is about fifteen degrees hotter than it was five seconds ago. I briefly consider fanning myself, but I stick my hands between my thighs instead. Before I do something stupid like reach for him.

He gives me a wicked smile. "Don't worry, I won't kiss you again until you ask me to. Besides, it's getting late, and we should get some sleep. The monsters will be up early."

Grateful I don't have to answer him right away, I get to my feet and tell him good night. When I'm safely in my room, I press the chilled beer bottle I'm still holding to my burning face. I can see why I fell for him in the first place. He's magnetic, and I'm drawn to him even though I know the smart thing would be to figure everything else out first. Getting tangled up with him would complicate everything for us both.

CHAPTER 13
ALEC

The alarm blares, and I blink blearily, disoriented at first. The last thing I can recall is a dream involving Tana, some whipped cream, and a pair of handcuffs. It had been a damn good dream. I'm so caught up in half-sleep that I even turn over to find her next to me, my hand searching through the sheets and blankets to find her soft, warm body, but all I find is cool emptiness. Then I remember. She's not here. She's in a room down the hall, and I'm alone in this bed.

I check my phone—eleven p.m.—and see a fire alert for the Battleboro High School gym—which most residents know affectionately as simply the "Old Gym." Part of the original high school built in the sixties, it's been more or less empty since the new campus was built the next block over. For most folks around here, it holds a lot of special memories from their old school days. Which explains why I was alerted even though it's my day off. If there's a fire at a place that amounts to a historical site in Battleboro, it'll be all hands on deck.

I quickly tug on my bunker gear, double-checking my med bag as I go. Still half asleep, I'm already dressed and in the kitchen chugging down an energy drink when Tana shuffles in, rubbing at her eyes. A couple things hit me at once.

First, she's wearing a pair of shorts that may as well be underwear. They flaunt her legs and hips to a degree I'm certain must be illegal in several states. I nearly choke on the energy drink.

A second thought hits me as the drink burns a path down my throat. I can't leave the kids alone here with her, that wouldn't be fair for either of them with everything still so new. Cursing under my breath, I dig out my phone and pray this won't be one of those nights Mom and Dad hit the wine bottle a little too hard and sleep like the dead. Mom isn't supposed to get the girls because I'm not on shift, so she wouldn't be planning to hear from me.

"Alec?" Tana says sleepily. "What's wrong?" She blinks several times in rapid succession, her eyes clearing as she takes me in. "Why are you dressed like that?"

I move to her, a bit awkward in the bulky material, and lift a hand to her cheek. The sleep clears from her eyes, and they dilate a little. Fuck if I don't love seeing her like this, all pliant and soft from sleep. I want nothing more than to sink into her warmth and feel her draped around me, even if it's only to fall asleep wrapped in her softness.

"I got a call out, baby. Trying to get ahold of my mom to

watch the girls. You can go back to sleep. Everything will be fine."

The call to Mom goes to voicemail. I curse under my breath as I try Dad's number with the same result. It's not required I show up, but a place like the Old Gym means everything to the residents of Battleboro. Zeke will want everyone there.

"What's a call out?" she asks, her voice still husky with sleep. Despite the alert still going off on my phone, the raspy sound to her voice has my cock hardening in my pants.

"Fire. They need everyone available to come out. Just waiting for one of my parents to answer so they can be here in case anything happens with the girls."

She hesitates, biting her lip, then says, "I can stay with them."

Dad's phone also goes to voicemail, but I'm not surprised. He could sleep through the apocalypse. "It's okay. I'll keep trying them." My hand drops from her cheek and rakes through my hair. Mom's phone goes to voicemail a second time.

Tana moves to the coffee machine, fighting a yawn, and puts a pod in to brew. "Don't be silly. They'll be asleep the whole time you're gone, I imagine. I can handle that. I'll keep trying your mom if you're worried about it, and as soon as she gets the call, she'll come help. You need to go."

My phone beeps again, and I hesitate. "Are you sure?"

"Positive," she answers as the scent of coffee wafts through the kitchen. "Go. I'll keep my phone on me if you need me. We'll be fine."

She was right when she said I'd have to start trusting her to make her own decisions. The girls know I often have to leave suddenly, and Tana is still their mother. I shoot out a text to my parents and decide to trust her.

"This shouldn't take long, maybe a couple hours. I'll be back as soon as I can. Call me if anything happens."

Tana nods and grabs her coffee from the machine. "I will."

I tug on my boots. "You can go back to sleep. It could be a long time before I get back."

"Stop stalling. You need to go. They'll be fine."

Getting to my feet, I move to open the door and then stop. I cross the space and tug her body close to me for one quick, hard kiss. "This doesn't count as a real kiss. I just can't leave without it."

Her eyes are dazed, and her chest is flushed when I force myself to turn away from her.

Zeke is first in the rig, already doing the 360-degree size up, which is a key factor in all fireground operations. The 360 assessment allows him to size up all areas of the structure to gain as much intelligence as possible to minimize the risk of death or injury to his firefighters. Sometimes, an arriving officer will try to take immediate action by running into the fire without an assessment. But on a structure like the gym, enclosed the way it is with few windows or doors in proportion to its size, it would mean a higher risk to the responding firefighters.

During his 360, Zeke would note any alternate points of entry—windows or doors—and any areas that may pose a hazard, such as downed power lines, propane tanks, or gas lines. He'll examine the structure for fire, cracks in the walls, or any other indication the roof may collapse. In this case, he already knows there isn't a basement. If he wasn't aware of the floor layout, the assessment would also help him formulate a best guess at the interior to determine how many probable rooms it contains.

When he's done, he meets me, the other responding volunteer firefighters, and the Battleboro Fire & Rescue crew at the Alpha, or address facing, side of the structure. But I don't need to hear his instructions. The fire has already fully engulfed the structure. There won't be any saving it. The most we can do is surround it with tankers and drown it out, protecting the structures and environment around it. It takes nearly a half-hour for mutual aid from the closest town to arrive with additional rigs to put out the blaze.

At one in the morning, I pull off my helmet and mask and wipe the streaming sweat from my face with a damp T-shirt I got from the rig. Walker is next to me, face flushed and ash-streaked, still glowing red from the heat of the fire. We observe the charred, soaked remains of the building with grim expressions.

"Shit," Walker says with a somber tone.

"That about sums it up," I say.

"Where's Captain?" he asks.

I nod to where Zeke is pacing. "On the phone with the fire marshal. May take a couple hours for them to show up."

Walker can only shake his head.

Arson.

I wouldn't have believed it if I hadn't seen the evidence myself. This wasn't any ordinary fire. There were signs of objects placed in front of the entrances to the gym, which would block the ability to fight the fire, and the sprinkler systems that remained operational had been tampered with. There was also evidence pointing to multiple points of origin.

Who in the world would want to burn down a place like the Old Gym? It has no other significance aside from being a place of fond memories for the people of Battleboro. Unless it was some kids doing dumb shit or playing a prank. But that's a hell of a prank.

Then Remy walks out, ashen and grim-faced. He sprays his face with water and says, "Found a body in the back. Must have been in a closet. Think it may have been some homeless person who camped out there. Cops get reports of people using the place for it all the time."

"Shit," Walker and I both say.

"You sure?" I ask.

"Damn near fell onto it, so I'd say yeah. I'm pretty fuckin' sure." Remy drinks deeply from his water bottle.

It's nearly three in the morning when we wrap up with cops and hand over the scene to the fire marshal to begin his investigation. Finding the body made a complicated night even more so. Not only had a landmark of Battleboro—one of the few remaining after the storm—been destroyed, but an innocent life had been taken.

You get desensitized to death by doing what I do, but some cases hit you right in the gut. For me, for whatever reason, this was one of them.

I climb into my truck, exhausted from exertion, lack of sleep, and emotionally wrecked. The first thing I do is check my phone, which I hadn't had the chance to glance at since I got to the scene.

1:15 a.m. Tana: Wasn't able to get ahold of your mom, but the girls are still asleep.

1:48 a.m. Tana: Gemma woke up and puked everywhere. Google says to clean her up and give her sips of Gatorade. We didn't have any Gatorade, so I gave her water.

2:13 a.m. Tana: She's crying that her stomach hurts and I didn't know what to do so we sat in a warm shower until she felt better.

2:15 a.m. Tana: Gemma fell asleep in the shower. I guess I'm stuck here.

2:37 a.m. Tana: Paisley just joined us in the bathroom and threw up all over the floor. I hosed her down in the shower.

2:48 a.m. Tana: Now they're both crying in the shower because hearing Paisley throw up made Gemma wake up and puke again

I'm equal parts worried and amused. I can almost hear Tana's voice from the text messages. I make a pit stop at a twenty-four-hour gas station and grab the necessities: Gatorade, ginger ale, popsicles, and saltine crackers. I won't be expected back at work for a few days, so we can hunker down for the duration of this stomach bug.

It's half past three by the time I pull into the driveway. The top floor lights are blazing bright, so I load up my arms with the bags of supplies and fight with the key in the dark.

When I get upstairs, I hear a low-throated moan coming from the girls' shared bathroom. I find the three of them curled up on the floor. Paisley and Gemma are on either side of Tana, their heads resting on her lap. She has one hand on each of their backs, rubbing soothing circles.

"Daddy," Gemma moans without moving so much as a muscle. "We don't feel good."

I kneel in front of them, taking in Tana's bruised under

eyes and pale complexion. "I see that, doll face. What happened?" I ask Tana.

"I think they got most of it out of their system. At least for now. Your parents never picked up. I tried them again, but the girls really weren't feeling well."

"Thank you for taking care of them. Sounds like everyone had a pretty rough night." I push back to my feet and wet two washcloths with cool water. The girls make identical sounds of relief when I press them to their foreheads. "Why don't we get you guys in bed, and we'll try to get some sleep?"

"What about school?" Paisley croaks.

I shake my head. "No school, sweet pea. Not until we make sure you're both all better."

"Is everything okay with you?" Tana asks softly so the girls don't hear as I help them to their feet. She stands and does a little stretch that does all kinds of intriguing things to her breasts underneath the thin cotton shirt.

"As well is it can be. I'll tell you more about it later." A pang of grief for the loss of the part of our relationship where she'd comfort me after a hard call hits me as I shuffle the girls to their room to change and brush their teeth.

Before Tana's accident, she would have tucked me into bed and wrapped her arms around me as I worked through the adrenaline crash after a call. Either that or got me a beer and gave me some space. She always seemed to know what I wanted. Right now, she's hovering in the doorway, uncertain of where she's supposed to be or what she's supposed to be doing.

"Thanks for helping with them," I tell her as the girls change. "You should get some sleep."

"You don't need me to sit with them? I'm sure you need to sleep too."

"I won't be able to sleep for a while. It'll take me time to settle, and my mom will be by once she sees how many calls she missed. She'll help so I can sleep then. Trust me, if this is a stomach bug, you'll want all the rest you can get if we all catch it."

Her eyes widen, and she nods. "Alright then. Good night, Alec," she says softly.

I give a curt nod when she doesn't push to stay like she would have before the accident. "Good night."

The sound of her footsteps fades as she pads down the stairs. I'd give anything to have her in bed with me as I settle our girls next to me for the rest of the long morning. Right now, she's downstairs, but she may as well be light-years away.

CHAPTER 14
TANA

It doesn't matter. It doesn't.

Ever since I woke up in that damn hospital bed, all I've wanted is for them to realize I'm not the woman they used to know. Right? So then why does it hurt so badly to remember how Alec looked at me? Like I was a stranger in his family.

A quick glance at the clock and the 2:00 a.m. readout mocks me. I groan into my pillow and toss and turn, trying to get comfortable, but to no avail. Every time I close my eyes, I see Alec's face before he told me to go back to bed. Defeat. He looked defeated. Like he couldn't fathom fighting another second despite the promises he'd made. Who can blame him? So far, the doctors have been right. I'm not going to remember anything from my former life. I've known that all along, and I thought I'd be relieved for Alec to finally get it, but I'm not.

It was only a matter of time before it happened, really. I just didn't expect it to hurt so much when it did.

Silly.

Groaning at the memory of the previous night plaguing me once again, I throw off the covers and pace at the foot of my bed. I'm not going to be able to sleep, again, so I go to the kitchen for something to distract me. Maybe they have some more of that cheesecake hidden in the fridge. The girls had been pretty much bed bound for the last twenty-four hours and Alec had been at their beck and call. I stuck to my room to give them their space and at Alec's request to make sure I didn't get the bug, too. They're all probably sleeping it off now that the worst of it has passed. I don't think Alec has slept much, if at all, in the past forty-eight hours.

But of course I find him sipping from a glass of amber liquid at the island in the kitchen. Based on his posture, I can tell it's not the first drink he's had. I glance at the bottle on the counter. It's nearly a third empty. How long has he been here, alone? I look back at him and study him more closely. His shoulders are slumped, and his eyes are deeply shadowed. When he glances up at me, I freeze. Maybe part of me is afraid he'll look at me like that again.

Like I don't belong.

He sighs heavily and sips from his glass. When he puts it down, his lips are glistening with the liquid. "Listen, I'm not in the mood to have a discussion right now." A little stung at the memory of *that look,* I turn, and then his voice hits my back. "But if you wanna have a drink with me, we can do that. No strings. It's always more fun to drink with someone else."

Rubbing my eyes, I cross to the wine rack in the island and take a bottle out at random. Maybe a fucking drink is exactly what I need. I don't know him; I don't know these kids. I barely know what the fuck I'm doing. I stop, bottle in hand, and glance around the empty kitchen. "Where the hell are the wine glasses?"

I'm so damn tired of not knowing anything. Of feeling like the odd man out. I'm so tired of agonizing about every little detail of my life. The thought of drinking all those worries away sounds sublime. Maybe he has the right idea.

Alec throws back the rest of his drink and gestures to a cabinet by the sink with his empty glass. Pushing to his feet, he moves wordlessly to the counter to mix another drink. The tang of bourbon and orange bitters fills the air. When he's done, he retrieves a corkscrew and holds out his hand for the bottle of wine. I give it to him, and he cuts the plastic off the top, uses the corkscrew to remove the cork, and pours a sample for me. The dark red liquid glimmers in the light from above.

I take the proffered glass. Look at it. Then hand the untasted wine back to him. "Don't be stingy, Alec. Fill 'er up." Might as well do the damn thing.

Am I imagining it, or does his sour expression melt into a grin for a half-second?

"Take it easy on that now. It's my favorite. But you should probably be careful. . . it's stronger than it seems."

I take a sip, unable to look away from him. The full-bodied flavor bursts on my tongue. I imagine him drinking it, and the thought of the wine on his tongue sends a shiver through me. Needing to get rid of the sudden burst of heat, I chug half the glass. At his lifted brow, I give a little shrug. "You aren't the only one who had a long couple days."

"Fair enough." He goes to sit back on his stool and drinks deeply. "I'm not gonna bite. Come sit down."

Swallowing hard, I take the stool next to him. "You okay?"

He cradles his glass on the counter in both hands. "Thought we weren't going to turn this into a discussion. We've done enough of that here recently, and it hasn't changed a damn thing. All I wanna do is forget. Can you give me that for one night?"

A rush of sympathy flows through me at the anguish in his eyes. I soften toward him a little and lift my glass. "Sure. I'm great at forgetting. What would you like to talk about instead?"

He thinks on it for a minute and then says, "Why don't we play a game?"

"You mean like a board game?"

Laughing a little, he says, "No, like a drinking game. It's called Never Have I Ever."

"How do you play?" I already regret this, and we haven't even started.

"Typically, whoever's turn it is will say something they've never done, and if you've done it, you take a drink."

I roll my eyes. "Well, that's impossible for me."

He nudges my shoulder. "I know. That's why you'll ask the questions, and I'll tell you if you drink or not."

I straighten. "Hey! What about you?"

"If I've done it, I'll drink."

"Fine." I chew on my lip as I think of something I want to know... about me, but mostly about him. The man I'm married to. "Never Have I Ever. . . been arrested."

He drinks, and I laugh incredulously. "Really? For what?"

Alec gestures with his glass. "You gotta drink, too, sweet pea."

My mouth falls open. "Me! Really? I've been arrested."

"Damn straight. In fact, I was arrested because of you."

"You're kidding."

"Nope. When we first started dating, this guy was hitting on you in a bar. You weren't into it, but he wouldn't take the hint. I intervened to tell him to back off, and he sucker-punched me. You got so pissed you threw your Fireball shot in his face, then cold-cocked him."

I drink a sip from my glass and shake my head. "Jesus. I'm afraid to ask anything else now."

"Don't be a chickenshit, Tee. Next question." The sound of the nickname coming from his mouth sobers me, but only a little. I like the sound of it. The familiarity.

Afraid he'll realize what he's said and take it back, I hurry on. "Never Have I Ever had a one-night stand." I bite my lip as I wait for his answer. I didn't intend to have the questions get so sexual right away, but wine apparently makes my mouth run away from me.

"Better drink up there, sweet pea." Alec bares his teeth in a grin and takes a sip.

"Really?" I ask.

"You were a heartbreaker."

"Bet you loved locking me down."

"Damn straight. Next question."

"Never Have I Ever cheated on someone."

Alec shakes his head. "Got me there. Next question." He doesn't take a drink either. I file that away in my ever-growing folder of facts about him. I didn't think he would be a cheater, but I was curious.

My heart begins to pound as I pluck up my courage. By this point, we're both pretty drunk, and, hey! I learned another new thing about myself—I can't drink for shit. "Do you remember how you said you wouldn't kiss me again until I made the first move?" I ask, dropping all pretense, filled with the courage from the alcohol.

Alec stills next to me, his jaw bunching and releasing. I want nothing more than to take another drink, but I can't. Maybe it's the wine or the events of the past day, but all I can think about right now is kissing him again. Tasting him along with the wine on my tongue. I know he'll be every bit as delicious and potent, and right now? That's all I crave.

He turns to me on the stool, spreading my thighs to make room for him. One of his hands is on the counter, bracing himself up. The other lifts to tug at my messy bun. "You trying to say you want to do more than kiss me, Tana?"

My throat is bone dry, and my tongue is stuck to the

room of my mouth. The room is spinning a little, but not so much that I don't know what I'm asking. All I can do is nod.

He shakes his head. "Gotta hear you say it. Tell me what you want."

I swallow hard. "I want you to kiss me."

The stool scrapes against the ground as he jerks mine closer to him. "I got that. But I'm pretty sure you said you want more than a kiss." I'm so hot I feel like I'm going to spontaneously combust. He nudges my knees farther apart with his. My hips ache, and I'm trembling.

"Uh-huh," is all I can get out.

"Or is it that you want me to kiss you here?" His hand presses over my sex. The thin silk shorts I'm wearing may as well be nonexistent. I'm afraid he can feel how wet I am beneath the material, but then he's kissing me.

A muffled sound is all I get out before the heat of his mouth seals over mine. Any protest I have is silenced by the thrust of his tongue. I go lax, melting against his hard body. A punch of heat hits me directly in the center of my belly, and I can't help the moan that slips from my lips. Damn my body. It wants him with a reckless abandon my mind simply can't comprehend.

He kisses me like I'm a craving he'll never satisfy. A thirst he'll never quench.

I could stop him. I know if I pushed hard enough, he'd move away, but the longer he kisses me, the harder it is to remember why we should stop.

I'm sure my lips are red and sore when he pulls back to whisper, "I bet you're so fucking wet for me, aren't you, sweet pea?" His fingers trace the thin material covering me. "Dripping."

All I can do is whimper. The ability for rational speech and thought has fled completely. No matter how much I know I should pull away from him and tell him he's not in the right frame of mind, the words simply won't form. This scenario is all kinds of wrong. Neither of us is thinking clearly.

Maybe that's what makes it right.

I'm tired of fighting with myself, with him. With my past or lack thereof. Tired of resisting.

I thread my fingers through his hair and use the grip on his skull to pull his lips back to mine.

What's left of his meager control snaps, and I get tossed on top of the counter, his big hands gripping my hips and canting them to cradle him between my thighs. The way he grinds his thick, hard erection against my clit has my fingers dropping to his shoulders to dig in, no doubt causing bruises underneath my grasp.

All I can think about, all I want, is to feel him inside me. There's an empty aching need to be filled. I'm mindless with it.

He breaks the kiss to growl, "Does that pretty pink pussy need me inside it?"

My eyes roll straight the hell into the back of my head. Sweet, kind, thoughtful Alec, who knows how to do pigtails and saves lives for a living, has a filthy, sinful mouth. He whispers those dirty words in my ear as he rocks his hips in a steady rhythm against me. Never quite fast enough to bring me to the edge, but enough of a tease that it drives me insane.

I'm afraid to open my mouth because I know I won't be able to stop begging if I do. He chuckles darkly, the scent of the bourbon giving me a heady high. Nipping at my lips, he says, "You don't have to answer. I can practically smell you already. I bet you're so sweet for me, aren't you? My dirty, sweet little angel. Do you want me to put my mouth on it?"

If I could climb inside him, I would. I can't seem to get close enough. He chuckles again and puts a hand to my throat, gliding it between my breasts. "Shhh, I'll take care of you. Lift your ass so I can lick you good."

He's a beautiful, filthy man with a wicked mouth.

I do as I'm told, and in five seconds flat, he has my silk shorts stripped off and my legs straight over his shoulders. I expect him to build up to it, tease me, but Alec spreads me wide with his fingers, baring it all to him, and buries his tongue deep inside.

"Oh fuck," I moan and clutch at his hair.

His big hands cup my ass cheeks and pull me closer. I don't know how the hell he's breathing, but he doesn't seem to care one way or another.

Then he's looking up at me and thrusting deep with his tongue. The sounds he's making fill my ears in a filthy cadence I don't think I'll ever forget, and it's that connection that sends me tipping over the edge. His rumble of approval has me biting down a scream. His hands clutch my trembling thighs, holding me close against his wicked tongue as I see stars.

CHAPTER 15
TANA

A loud, childish shriek has me bolting upright and immediately regretting the action. Flopping onto my back, I press a hand to my throbbing head and wince at the sunlight streaming in the window. I crack open an eyelid when my brain doesn't feel like it's being trampled by a herd of angry wildebeests.

The first thing I notice is that I'm not in my room.

What the fuck.

The second thing I notice is that I'm not alone.

What the fuck.

A distinct, tattooed forearm wraps around my waist and pulls me against a warm, *naked* chest. Lips nuzzled at my throat for a moment, followed by light snores. A quick glance over my shoulder reveals Alec wrapped around me like ivy on a pole. And if I'm not mistaken, there's a very generous erection pressed firmly against my ass.

My naked ass.

WHAT THE FUCK.

As carefully as possible, I slip out from under Alec's arm. Thankfully, he's practically dead to the world from staying up all night at work, then tending to the girls until they could stop throwing up, then getting hammered and having me for dessert. He's been a busy guy.

After throwing on a pair of boxers and a T-shirt I find in his dresser drawer, I sneak out of his room. I can't find *any* of my clothes, but I'll worry about that later. I have to make it to my room without running into the girls. They don't need to be any more confused than they already are. Luckily the coast is clear, and I sprint to my room and lock the door behind me.

I hop in the shower and hope a cold blast of water will clear my head, but all it does is make me squeal out a curse. Minutes later, I leap out colder, more irritable, and still as tired as before. I dress in a pair of yoga pants and a thin, soft T-shirt that swings around my hips. All my old clothes appeared in my closet at some point, and I decided not to say anything about it. I've got bigger things to worry about than clothes.

Like what the hell else I did with Alec last night.

I'm in the kitchen a short while later, trying to act as normal as possible before the girls come down the stairs, when a key turns in the front door lock, and a woman bursts through in a whirlwind of cheetah print and hairspray. My mouth drops open, and I'm at a loss for words. She's a good six inches shorter than me and as petite as I am full-figured.

Her eyes widen momentarily when she catches sight of

me, and then her mouth splits into a wide, red lipstick-covered smile. "Well, I'll be, Tana honey. It sure is great to see you." She crosses the living room to me and wraps me in a cloud of perfume. "I've been meaning to come by and see you sooner, but Alec was adamant I not bug you too much. I tried to tell him I wouldn't be a bother, but he's damn protective, isn't he? You gotta love him. I'm so sorry I missed your calls and messages. Frank and I got into a bottle of Sauvignon Blanc and passed out after binging *Criminal Minds*. How are the girls?"

"You must be Alec's mom," I say.

She makes a sympathetic face and pats my arm. "I'm sorry, honey, I don't know what I was thinking. Sometimes my mouth just runs away from me. Yes, I'm Tracy Dorran. I guess I should have led with that."

"It's okay. Nice to meet you again?" I say, the end of the sentence tilting up in question. "They're all sleeping right now. We've had a long couple days with the fire and a stomach bug."

Tracy moves to the kitchen island. "I've got just the thing. Best chicken soup my granny ever made. It could cure broken bones. I'll get it cooking so it's ready for them when they can keep food down. Why don't you sit with me a spell, and we can get to know each other?"

"Don't you already know me?" I say, uncertain if I'm confused or just tired.

"Well, I knew you before the accident, but I don't know you now, and you sure don't know me. It'll be fun to get reacquainted."

She gets coffee going and a heavenly-smelling soup on the stove. Soon, she places a cup of coffee in front of me. I don't know what it is, but it tastes better than anything I've ever made. What does she put in this that makes it taste so damn good?

Her directness is refreshing. Since the accident, most of the people I've met have eyes full of pity and don't have a damn thing to say. I find myself relaxing in her presence and breathing deeply for the first time since I got out of bed.

"I'd like that," I say as Tracy moves around the kitchen, whipping up breakfast and chicken soup with a practiced hand.

An hour later, Gemma makes her appearance, her sleepy eyes peering around the corner of the stairs, wide with curiosity. Both of the girls had been up and down catching up on sleep. "Gramma!" she says when she realizes who is in the kitchen with me. Leaping across the distance, she barrels into Tracy's legs.

"Hey there, punkin'. How are you feeling?" She rubs a hand over Gemma's head.

"A little better. My tummy still feels a little wobbly."

"Why don't I make you a nice, cold glass of ginger ale? That should help settle your tummy."

Suddenly, Gemma pushes away from Tracy's legs and throws herself bodily in my direction. I only manage to catch her at the last second. "I want Mama!" She wails and clings to my thighs. My frantic eyes meet Tracy's over the counter.

I'd managed by the skin of my teeth with them. Mostly because I was running on instinct, and the girls were distracted by how exhausted and terrible they felt. I kept them clean and alive, so I figured that was pretty good. At least, that's what I thought until Alec came home and gave me that look.

The memory of it in the forefront of my mind keeps me frozen as Gemma's little body presses close to mine. My hands hover in the hair, unsure if I should lay them on her shoulders or pat her head. "What do I do?" I mouth to Tracy.

"Hug her," Tracy mouths back.

An internal battle wages for a few long seconds. I don't know what the hell I'm doing. But there's also *something* inside me that won't let me leave this little girl wanting. She needs me, maybe as much as I need an anchor tethering me somewhere, anywhere. So I wrap my arms around her little frame and provide comfort as well as receive it.

My eyes close, and there's a stirring inside my brain. . . and maybe my heart. Muscles soften and relax, and the little girl's scent of shampoo and sugar fills my nose. My brain may not remember her, but I think maybe. . . I think maybe my heart does. She gives in to me, snuggling closer, and I let her, rubbing a soothing hand on her back.

"It's okay, Gemma," I say into her hair. "I'm still here."

She shudders against my legs. "I thought you were going to leave me again. I woke up, and you weren't there."

I slump against her, my heart breaking a little. "I'm sorry, sweetheart. I didn't go anywhere. I'm not going anywhere."

"I don't want you to go," she whispers. I think I may have preferred if she'd screamed it at me. But she says it like it comes from the deepest wells of her fears. And rightfully so, considering what this precious little soul has been through.

All I can say is, "I'm right here." Because while the sudden urge to protect her at all costs is the strongest thing I've felt since I woke up, I also have Alec's words warning me not to make any promises I can't keep.

Clearly sensing the tension, Tracy swoops in with a stack of pancakes for me and a fresh glass of ginger ale for Gemma. "Sip on this, sugar, and let's see how your tummy tolerates it this morning."

"Okay, Gramma," Gemma says sweetly and climbs onto the barstool next to me.

She's got a little more color to her, which, according to my frantic internet searching, must be a good sign. It must have been some freak twenty-four-hour bug. Poor babies. Hard to believe I used to do this every day with both girls when I can barely keep it together for myself now.

"What have you got planned today?" Tracy asks as she rinses off her breakfast dishes.

"I'm not sure, really. I guess I'm at loose ends, trying to figure out who I am now and what I'm supposed to be doing."

"Why don't you take my car and go out for a little while? Alec mentioned you got the all-clear to drive. I'll help Alec with the girls. It sounds like you can use some fresh air."

"I don't know. . ."

"Don't you argue with me now. You can't spend all your time cooped up here waiting on your life to fall back into your lap. From what Alec told me, the doctors don't even think your memories are going to come back. Which means you have to figure out your new way forward, and the only way you can do that is to get started."

"But what if I can't—"

Tracy levels me with a look, and I see where Alec gets his iron sense of will. "Can't never could no nothin', little girl. Now get out of here."

It's not until I'm in the car and driving around Battleboro that I realize I have no idea where I'm supposed to be going. I just didn't want to face Tracy's wrath by telling her that. After driving around for a while, I find myself at the park by the river where Alec kissed me. I didn't even realize that's where I was going until I'm out of the car and sitting at the picnic bench under a tree.

Thumping my head against the table as though it'll rattle the memories out, I try to get a hold of myself. I've been waiting for my next step to hit me in the head when that may never happen. Like Dr. Rennen said, my memories may *never* come back. It's time to figure out what that'll mean for my future.

First: I need to figure out a job.

I know Alec would let me leech off him forever. It's just the kind of guy he is, but that's not who I am. I need to support myself and have the freedom that provides should things go south.

Second: I need to figure out what to do about the girls. It's not fair to them to be wishy-washy in their lives. I need to decide once and for all if I want to put in the work to be there for them or to bow out now.

Which leads me to the third thing: what to do about Alec.

That may be the most difficult of them all. My body tells me yes. Clearly, it has no trouble remembering him. It screams at me to beg for more kisses, more touches. . . more, more, more.

But I'm terrified that he only wants his wife back, not *me*. And what happens when he snaps out of his grief and realizes we're not the same.

Not anymore.

I couldn't handle it if he were to push me away. So, for now, I won't do anything about Alec. I'll focus on the first two points of my plan and move from there.

Feeling decidedly better, I push to my feet when a high-pitched sound catches my attention. I look for the source when movement catches my eye. A gasp bursts from my chest when a little black head lifts from a bed of grass a couple dozen yards away. It's a cat, a beautiful, dark tortoise-shell, I think. God only knows how I remember what *that's* called and not anything important. Stupid brain.

The cat gets to its feet and begins moving toward me slowly and off-centered. Then I realize its front legs are deformed. They can't extend fully, so the poor thing is a limping, hoping mess all the way over to me. When it gets close enough, I realize it's all skin and bones. It can't weigh more than a couple pounds if that.

"Oh my god," I exclaim as I drop to my knees. "What happened to you?"

Its responding mewl is pitiful, and I hesitate to pet it,

worried it may have been hit by a car, which is why its legs are so deformed. But it presses against my legs and doesn't seem to be in pain. I don't know if that's better, though, because that would mean its legs had healed like this.

I gently pull it into my lap, its purrs vibrating in my chest. "Did someone leave you here?" A spurt of anger heats my veins. It presses its head into my wrist, and I look around as though I'll find answers, but there are none. "What are we going to do with you?"

My mind races for a few minutes before I think to pull my phone out of my pocket. I do a quick Google search and find a local rescue. I hit the call button with the cat curled happily in my lap as though it's where it's always belonged.

Ten minutes later, I'm pulling up in the rescue's front parking lot. It's a little rundown building with dozens of cages in the back. A cacophony of dogs barking greets my ears as I gingerly retrieve the cat and head inside.

A bank of chairs is to my immediate right, and an unmanned desk blocks off the rest of the room. The din from the dogs is buffered, but not much. The cat seems to know it's found a friend because it snoozes happily in my arms. Meanwhile, I'm still frantic at the thought of it being hurt.

A woman blows in with a kitten in her lab coat pocket. It peeks out over the edge, scents the cat in my arms, and dives back down. The woman searches the desk for something and, not finding it, blows out a breath that moves the sweep of bangs from in front of her eyes. Seeing me, she offers a kind, if a bit harried, smile. "Sorry for the wait. We had a bit of an emergency. I'm Penelope Baker. You can call me Penny. How can I help you?"

I hold up the cat. "This girl needs some help. At least, I'm pretty sure it's a girl. It just showed up at the park where I was at. I didn't know what else to do."

Penny's bright blue eyes widen, and she moves around the desk to motion with a hand to the hallway. "Oh my goodness. Poor thing. Let's go to the back, and we'll take a look."

I follow a step behind Penny to the exam room. "Do you think she'll be okay?"

She places the cat on the table and makes soothing noises as she begins her examination. The cat, who doesn't seem to know a stranger, is instantly friendly and butts her head against Penny's hands, audibly purring. "It is a she, and she seems to be doing as okay as possible. Probably starving and dehydrated, and there's definitely something going on with her front legs. We'll have to get an X-ray and run some tests, but it's good that you brought her in. She wouldn't have made it long in the world like this."

"I didn't know what else to do," I repeat.

Penny notices my nerves and gives me a comforting smile. "It'll be okay, Tana. We'll take care of her."

I give a start at the sound of my name. "You know me? I'm sorry, I didn't even think of that." I probably should have known, considering how small Battleboro is. Even during my time walking around or when we went to the grocery store, people would give me a friendly wave like they knew me— and they probably did.

Penny moves around the room with practiced ease, drawing up vaccines and dispensing medication to the cat, who isn't pleased but is placated with treats. "We know each other in passing. It's a small town, and my brother Rhett's best friend Jaxon works with Alec."

Shaking my head, I say, "I don't think I'll ever get over meeting people who know more about me than I do about myself."

She sticks her pencil into the bun of messy blonde waves on the top of her head, pushes up her glasses, and sticks out a hand. "Well, why don't we pretend we just met. I'm Penelope Baker. You can call me Penny. I'm a veterinarian and run the rescue with a couple other volunteers. It's nice to meet you."

I can't think of anything other than, "I am Tana Dorran, and that's about it," as I shake hers.

"C'mon, you can do better than that."

"I'm Tana. I like true crime shows, gardening, and I've got the biggest crush on my husband." Saying it out loud makes me give a nervous giggle. "But don't tell him that yet."

Penny mimes zipping her lips. "Nice to meet you, Tana." She gestures to the cat stretching on the exam table. "This little girl looks to be about two or three years old. I'm going to bet her legs are from a birth defect. But let's take those X-rays to be sure. We'll keep her here for observation for a bit while we run some tests."

I hesitate and then say, "Do you mind if I stick around while you do? I won't be able to relax until I know she's okay. Sad to say, but I have a lot in common with this cat."

"Of course! You can hang out as long as you don't mind

lending a hand. We can always use the help, I'm afraid. I can't seem to say no to any stray that shows up, and I have more animals than helpers these days."

My spirits lift a little. "Really? Honestly, I could use the distraction."

Penny nods enthusiastically. "I'm happy to put you to work."

For the first time since I woke up in the hospital, I start to feel at home in my own skin.

ALEC

The memory of her sweetness is still on my tongue when I finally wake up. I must have slept like the dead because I don't find her in bed with me. I'd broken down some of those barriers around her when she'd exploded under my mouth. Giving her space will only give her enough time to build them back up.

With that on my mind, I get dressed quickly to find her and check on the girls. Much as I want to head straight to her room, my priorities are Gemma and Paisley. I find them in the living room with my mom, but no Tana.

"Is Tana up yet?" I ask Mom, trying not to seem too eager.

"I sent her out to take a break. It looked like she needed it." Mom gives me a pointed look.

She wants to chew me out, I can tell, but I ignore the bait. "Thanks for coming over to help. We didn't get much sleep last night."

Mom's expression shifts. "I heard about the fire. Any news?"

"Not yet. The state fire marshal is investigating it as a possible arson."

Mom shakes her head and clucks her tongue. "That's crazy. Who would want to burn down that old thing? It's not worth anything."

"Could be a lot of reasons." I tip my head to the girls who have stopped listening to the movie they're watching and are now paying close attention to us. "We'll talk about it later. How are you girls feeling?"

Both are eating a pile of crackers and sipping on sports drinks. Gemma is the first to perk up. Of course. "I feel a whole lot better, Daddy."

Paisley slams back into her nest of pillows. "I'm so tired," she says.

"Why don't you ladies rest, and I'll clean up the explosion from upstairs."

Now that the interesting conversation is over, their attention goes back to the movie. I nod at my mom and head back upstairs to deal with the mountains of laundry. How do we go through every sheet and towel in the house every time they have a stomach bug? It doesn't make sense. It's up there with the physics of losing socks in dryers and never having enough hair ties. #GirlDad.

I get the first set of sheets and towels in the washer and finally get myself in the shower. I groan as soon as I step beneath the hot spray. The scalding water feels fantastic on my sore muscles, and the last twenty-four hours of sweat and grime sluice down the drain.

It's then that I allow my thoughts to drift back to her. Although they're never far away. I imagine her bent over as she was in the garden and then spread before me on the counter. My cock hardens instantly. I let my head drop back into the spray and try to think of anything else, but the images are burned into my brain.

If this were any other day, any other time, I'd be able to resist the need to grip my hard length in one fist, but with running on no sleep and my need for her at a fever pitch, resistance is a thing of the past. A breath hisses out of my lungs as I stroke myself and think of all the ways I would have shown her my appreciation if she'd been in bed with me when I woke up.

I imagine her on her hands and knees on the bed in front of me, ass up in the air. Her cheeks spread wide for me, teasing me with a glimpse of her wet, swollen femininity. She would arch her back and make that little sound in the back of her throat that drives me crazy. I groan again at the thought of it. My dick becomes impossibly hard underneath my stroking hand. The sounds of the shower and my surroundings fade away as I imagine her moving her ass against me. I would tangle her hair in one hand and pull it back as I teased my cock against the entrance to her pussy. She'd make a desperate sound, and that's when she'd start begging. Damn, but I love the sound of her begging.

My hand strokes harder as my breath comes in desperate pants. This isn't gonna take long, I can tell already. Just like I know it wouldn't take long if I ever get my hands on her again. I've missed her. So fucking much. Last night wasn't nearly enough to sate how much I want her.

I'm not even embarrassed that the thought of pushing my hard cock inside her wet heat has me coming all over my hand. A sound rips from my chest, and I slap my forearm on the wall to keep myself upright. The orgasm is quick and ruthless. Not nearly enough to slake all the desires I have inside me, but enough to clear my head. At least for now.

I finish the shower with an efficiency born from habit. I wash my hair, scrub off the last twenty-four hours, and get dressed.

I know I fucked up pushing Tana away the way I did. It probably hurt her feelings, and she didn't deserve it. She hadn't done anything wrong. It was me. Just because this is hard on everyone doesn't give me the right to take it out on her. Besides, we need to talk about what happened the night before.

When I'm dressed, I get fresh sheets and make all the beds. I don't know what it is about a fresh, clean bed that makes me feel better, but as soon as they're done, I'm reassured. Tana used to do all this stuff for us. She practically decorated the whole house and couldn't seem to go a month without changing something around or finding another perfect accessory.

Mom takes the girls for some change of scenery—and to give Tana and I some time together. After that feverish shower, I probably should have asked them to stay, but Gemma and

Paisley desperately needed to work off some of their returning energy. I spend the next hour cleaning up the carnage from the night before, switching over laundry, and scarfing down a bowl of Mom's homemade chicken noodle soup. By the time I hear the front door creep open, I feel almost human again.

I stride into the living room, fully intent on delivering an award-worthy apology. Then, I'm going to grovel. And if that fails, I'm gonna convince her to let me have a taste of her again until she forgives me. Except the sight of her stops me in my tracks.

"What in the holy hell is that?" I ask, eyeing the ball of patchy fur in her hands with trepidation. It lifts its head, revealing glowing yellow-orange eyes, and I frown. "Is that a cat?"

"Don't be mad," she says and cuddles the purring mass closer to her chest. Great, now I'm jealous of a cat.

"I'm not mad," I say softly. I consider bringing up what happened between us but set it aside for now.

"It's a stray and doesn't have anyone else. She needs a place to stay while I figure out a home for her." Her eyes are big and bright. Even if I were going to say no to her—which, let's face it, rarely happens—the look of desperation in her eyes would have swayed me. I'd give her anything—every-thing—at this point.

"You don't have to convince me. This is your house too. You don't need my permission." I move closer to pet its soft fur. Giving her a wry smile, I say, "You realize once the girls see you've brought a cat home, they're going to riot. You'll be lucky if you can convince them to let it leave if you do find another home for her."

She groans. "I didn't even think of that, oh my god. What are we going to do?"

"Why don't we start with cleaning her up some, and you can tell me what happened."

"And the doctor says we can either leave the leg the way it is and deal with the disability or schedule a consult with an orthopedic surgeon, which could be expensive." Tana is nearly out of breath as she rambles on after we dry off a very distressed cat. "I'm sorry again about springing this on you. I should have called and asked first, but I didn't even think about it. I didn't know what else to do, and I couldn't leave her to starve."

Her eyes plead for me to understand, but she doesn't need to explain anything to me. She may not remember her past, but the woman she used to be would have done the same thing. My wife has always had a heart of gold and would give the shirt off her back to someone if they needed it.

"Looks like she's in luck. Have you decided on a name yet?"

Tana blinks owlishly at me. "I didn't get that far," she admits with a laugh. "Maybe we should let the girls decide?"

"Probably a good idea. They've always wanted a pet."

The cat settles into Tana's lap, tail wrapping possessively

around her wrist as it begins to purr. Tana studies me. "Why didn't we ever get one?" she asks.

I lean against the door frame and lift my other shoulder. "Never enough time, I guess. Since we had the girls back-to-back, you had your work, and I'm not home all the time, it never seemed like the right moment to commit to something else."

As she runs a hand over the cat's back, she says, "Seems pretty hectic."

"Yeah, I guess so. We always seemed to like it that way." But there isn't a lot of conviction in my voice. My thoughts go back to the night of her accident, and my stomach sours with regret. Did we always like it so busy, or did we simply let our commitments become more important than every-thing else? More important than each other?

"And you're sure we can keep her? I don't want to incon-venience you."

I cross to her and lift her chin, setting aside the urge to press the pad of my thumb over her lower lip. "You're not an inconvenience. Why don't you get some blankets from the closet for her? We'll make up a bed in the laundry room where she'll be nice and toasty and comfortable. Did you get food for her?"

"It's in my car," she says. "Our closet?"

The urge to kiss her is overwhelming, but I don't want to push her again. Not yet. So I merely nod and retrieve the food, dishes, and litter box from the car. There are also toys, catnip, and a scratching post. I carry the lot of it to the laundry room at the back of the house. I'm filling up the water dish when I hear Tana's footsteps in the hallway.

"Did you get enough stuff for her?" I tease as I stoop to put the water dish next to the food bowl. Turning, I find Tana holding the cat in the doorway, her face ghost white.

My heart falls to my feet. "What's wrong?" I move to her. "Baby, what is it? Are you hurt?"

"Why didn't you tell me?" she asks.

And then I realize.

She knows.

CHAPTER 17
TANA

The cat wiggles once it scents the food, so I set her down on the floor with numb hands, my heart pounding in my ears. Frustration has my thoughts in a jumble—even more so than they usually are. I close my eyes to try to focus. A headache brews in my temples.

"Did you remember?" comes Alec's breathless voice.

My gaze shoots to his. "No, I don't remember. You need to accept my memories aren't going to come back like that." I snap my fingers. Throwing the paperwork on the dryer next to me, I bite out, "I found this in the closet. Explain it to me, Alec, because unless I'm mistaken, what I'm reading is that I—*we*—miscarried after the accident. Why didn't you tell me?" The hurt I feel is so complex it feels like my insides have been scraped raw. "Is it because you think I wouldn't care? That it wouldn't matter to me?"

Alec may as well have been made of stone. "Babe, no. That's not why at all."

He tries to move closer, but I take a step back. He freezes in place, his eyes hurt and pleading. "Don't call me that. I'm not your babe. I thought we were going to be honest. Did you want me to remember on my own?"

His hair stands straight up because he constantly runs his hands through it. "I don't have the perfect answers for you. I should have told you before now, but Tana, I only just got you back. There never seemed to be a right time."

"Of course there isn't a right time to tell me something like that." The maelstrom of emotion coursing through me makes my chest ache. "But if I had to guess, it would have been right away."

He goes quiet, and he visibly deflates. "You're right."

"Then tell me now. Tell me everything right now, Alec, or I walk."

He gives a stiff, jerky nod and moves to his bedroom. The paperwork and photos are sprawled out on the bed where I'd left it in a panic after finding them in the closet. I'd been pulling down a blanket from the top shelf when the box came tumbling down with it. Inside the box—which I didn't notice the first time around—is a strip of ultrasound pictures, a half a dozen pregnancy tests, a stuffed bunny, and a well-worn onesie. These items don't mean anything to me, but I find my heart clenching at the sight of them.

Alec slumps on a chair, looking forlorn, his posture weighted down with his emotions. "This was your keepsake box. We'd been trying to have another baby for a few months now. You were so excited when you got the positive test that you took about twenty of them and kept every single one. I was hesitant at first about starting over—that's why I had been signing up for so many shifts at the time of your accident. We're doing fine financially, but the thought of adding another kid to the mix made me realize I don't want to just be doing fine. I want to give my family everything." He sighs and puts everything back in the box, nudging it in my direction. "You'd been spotting for weeks, and at first, our midwife said it was probably normal. It happens sometimes, but I think you knew something was wrong. I could just tell. You seemed so nervous about this pregnancy, and you never had been before.

"That night, you called me at work to touch base, and everything was fine. We were cautiously optimistic about the pregnancy, even though it also terrified me. Later on, you knew something was wrong because you tried calling me over and over, but I was busy on another call and missed it. You were driving yourself to the ER when you were hit. After that, when you were taken to the hospital, I found out our baby was gone. I was afraid I was going to lose you too. It was the worst night of my life, bar none."

"How far along was I?" I press a hand to my belly, trying to imagine a life growing there. I don't know what to feel. I should be sad, but it's clouded by the anger of having something so fundamental kept from me.

"Eleven weeks." He hands me the ultrasound photos. "These were from eight weeks or so."

I squint my eyes at the swipes of shadows and white space. If it weren't for a little arrow pointing to a section with a heart rate strip at the bottom, I wouldn't have even known what I was looking at. A knot forms in my throat. I'd already lost so much. . . so much. This, on top of everything else and combined with Alec keeping it from me, has the tears I've been holding back spilling over.

"I'm so sorry, Tana. I have no excuse for not telling you other than I selfishly thought I was protecting you. I didn't want you to think it was your fault or keep you from making any progress in healing." His head dips. "To be honest, I was also grieving the loss, and it felt like if I said it out loud, it would make it real. Too real. I'd lost the baby, and I didn't want to lose you too if you found out and decided it was too much for you." He lets out a ragged breath. "It was wrong of me. I shouldn't have kept something so important from you. I won't do it again. I promise you."

And I can tell he means his words. The conviction in his voice and the certainty in his eyes are undeniable. I close my eyes against the waves of hurt and try to put myself in Alec's shoes. He would have been facing the possibility of a life as a single dad raising Gemma and Paisley on his own. All without his wife and their future child.

Had he even had time to grieve his loss? For the baby who hadn't made it and the wife he knew who might never come back?

I didn't think so. When would he have had the time?

I sit on the bed next to him, our shoulders brushing. "I didn't think things could get any worse. When I saw the discharge paperwork, it was like I'd been punched in the gut. I guess things can always get worse."

He lets out a shaky breath. "They can also get better. I still have you. I'll do whatever it takes to keep you."

"But I—"

"No buts," Alec says firmly. "I can't give you back the baby we lost or make your memory better, but I can show you why I'm the man for you. Why I've always been the man for you. If you'll let me."

My chest aches. "I don't know if I can be the woman for you, though."

He puts a hand to my cheek, and for a moment, I think he's going to kiss me. But he only smooths it over my hair, then down my back. "You're enough just as you are." He leans forward and touches his forehead to mine. "I'm sorry for hurting you, for keeping that from you. It won't happen again. I promise you that. Can you believe me?"

"No more secrets, okay? I need to know everything. Is there anything else you aren't telling me about the accident? That night?" He shakes his head no, then stops. "What is it?" I ask. God, what else could there be?

"The man who crashed into you?"

I furrow my brows. "The drunk driver?"

Alec nods. "He was our next-door neighbor's son. Leon? You may have met him. Kid was only nineteen. Not even old enough to drink, but he'd been out with some buddies and thought he'd be okay to go home."

A memory comes back—nothing from before the accident but of the man banging on the door when Alec was at work. I tell him about the interaction with the drunk and his daughter. "Who was that?" I ask.

"Leon. The kid's father." Alec curses under his breath. "I'll talk to him. He shouldn't be bothering you. He hasn't been around here anymore since then, has he?" Alec asks.

"No, just that one time. Is he someone I should be worried about?"

"I'll talk to him," he repeats. "I doubt he'll give you more trouble aside from occasional benders. I can have one of the guys from work drive by when I'm on shift to make sure you're okay."

I scoff and roll my eyes at him. "I don't need a babysitter. I'm sure it'll be fine. He's probably just distraught about losing his son like that. It can't be easy."

Alec thumbs my lip, his eyes heating as he stares at them. He gives himself a little shake. "That's no excuse for scaring you like that. Not after what you've been through. Let me do this, Tana, or I'll go crazy. Please."

I start to argue again, but then I notice his hands are trembling, so I swallow back the words. "Thank you."

It's then I notice the dark circles smudged under his eyes which droop with fatigue. The normally clear, bright gray is abnormally dull. He looks so tired. Worn ragged. Had he looked like this the entire time? It hadn't occurred to me how much strain he must be under. But learning he'd lost a baby and the woman who used to be his wife undoes me and breaks down some of the walls between us. He's shouldered that burden alone to shield me. A thick, heavy knot rises in my throat, and hot tears sting my eyes and the back of my nose.

When he relaxes a little next to me, I hesitate, then lean

close to him and wrap my arms around his big shoulders. He stills with my touch until he realizes I'm hugging him. Then his big arms are wrapping around me in return, enveloping me in his warmth. He tucks my head into his neck, and I sink into his heat.

It feels good to be held—protected—but what I love even more is how he relaxes against me. How his body gravitates closer, trying to be as near to me as possible. He trembles on a long, deep inhale like he's been starved of this for so long, and he'll die without it. My eyes flutter closed. I feel like I'm enjoying someone else's man and the guilt gnaws at me a little. But he feels too good to let go.

I'm awestruck by how much he clearly cared about his wife and family. He must have loved her—me—so much to have put up with everything that's happened. I was a lucky woman to have that kind of devotion.

He pulls back reluctantly and tucks my hair behind my ear. "Why don't we just start over? From the beginning."

"Why?"

"Because I don't think I've been fair trying to push you to get your memories back. It hasn't been fair keeping such a big secret from you. Hell, I haven't given you space to figure out what you want, and that's really the only thing that matters."

My heart thuds heavily in my chest. "What are you saying?" Is he going to suggest we strip down and get naked again? I mean, I don't think I'd be mad about it, but. . .

"I'm just saying, why don't we go out and do something fun? Something that has nothing to do with your memories or the accident or anything else. I think we both could use some fun time where we don't have to think too much."

I smile a little shyly. "Are you asking me on a date, Mr. Dorran?"

And I think I fall a little in love with him when he grins and says, "That depends on if your answer's yes."

CHAPTER 18
ALEC

"I can't thank you enough for taking the girls again. I really appreciate how flexible you've been with us. I don't know what I would've done without you."

Mom beams at me and waves away my gratitude. "I am their grandmother. That's what I'm here for. You two go out and have fun. You deserve it."

"I'll bring you back something to go."

"That'll be fine. Take as long as you need. All night, even."

I roll my eyes. "Mom, don't even start."

She giggles and hustles the girls out the door. They, of course, put up quite a protest considering they have a new cat to play with but eventually leave. Tana is in our bedroom getting ready. My palms are suddenly sweaty, and my knees feel weak. It's almost like our first date all over again.

I figured I'd keep it simple. I'm taking her to a restaurant near the beach with amazing food and a gigantic aquarium.

We used to go there all the time, but it feels like tonight is the first time. And in a way, it kind of is. I never thought I'd see the amnesia as a blessing in disguise, but I can't deny I'm enjoying falling for my wife all over again.

Heels click softly against the floor, and I turn to find Tana stepping into the kitchen. She's wearing a classic black dress with a deep V neckline. And that's as far as I get because her tits look fantastic. I nearly swallow my own tongue looking at her. When the lump in my throat dissolves, I choke out, "Maybe we shouldn't go out."

Her lips quiver a little as she smiles. "What do you mean? Is something wrong?"

"The only thing wrong is that I'm not taking that dress off you right now."

"Alec!" she squeaks out.

Grinning, I say, "Well, I promised I'd be honest. And the truth is all I want to do is take it off you." She's frozen in the doorway, and there's a moment of delicious tension where I almost give in, say fuck it, and take her to bed. But we both need to connect on more than the physical level. I want to take her out, treat her nice, and then bring her home and do dirty things to her. "But we'd better leave because I promised you a date."

The newfound tension between us is electric on the short drive to the restaurant. I can't stop staring at her legs. Or her tits, really. My eyes seem to ricochet from one to the other the whole drive there. We're lucky we make it there in one piece.

We make small talk on the drive to the restaurant, but I

don't remember a damn word. We're in line to be seated when a high-pitched squeal cuts through our little bubble. Tana instinctively moves closer to me, and I wrap my arm around her waist and pull her flush against my side as we follow the sound.

Her head twists around to see where the noise comes from, and we see a sharply dressed older woman with vibrant red hair and a gigantic smile. Her teeth are so white and perfect that I do a double-take.

"Oh my God, Gary! I told you that was her. As I live and breathe, it's Tana! From The Purple Cat!" The woman beelines for us and takes out her phone. "Can I get a selfie with you? My girlfriends won't believe me when they learn I met the real Tana Dorran. We just love your stuff. Do you ever think you'll open up the site again?"

Tana visibly freezes. Her expression goes blank. I immediately want to put her behind me, protect her. When I move to do so, she puts a hand on my arm. We share a look, and I back off.

She recovers quickly and gives the woman a sweet smile. "That's so kind of you. I don't have any plans to reopen in the immediate future. Unfortunately, I'm still dealing with health issues, as I'm sure you understand."

The woman's discerning eyes flicker to the pink scar on Tana's forehead. "Bless your heart. In all my excitement, I totally forgot about your accident. I feel so silly."

Tana gives her a gentle smile. "You don't have to apologize. I'd be happy to take a picture with you if you want one."

The woman brightens again. "I'd love that!" She pulls

Tana close and hands me the camera to take a photo. Tana looks a little wary, but the woman seems satisfied when I snap a couple of pictures.

"I'll keep my eye out for your announcement when you want to open the store again. We all wear your stuff."

"You have a good night now," Tana says kindly without answering.

The woman's husband gestures impatiently from where he stands by the hostess stand. A waitress leads the pair of them away, and I can feel Tana relax next to me.

"You okay?" I run a hand down her arm and intertwine her fingers with mine.

"Yeah, I'm fine. That just took me off guard. People have recognized me before, I assume because they've seen me around, but I haven't been recognized because of my social media presence. It's strange. Did people really recognize me before like that?"

"Not often, but sometimes. Especially people around the area because it's not a huge place."

Our names are called, and we're seated at a secluded booth near the aquarium. After the waitress takes our drink order, she watches the fish for a while. It hits me then—she's nervous.

"Have you thought about what you want to do about the site?" I'll admit I've been curious. It had been such a huge passion of hers before the accident.

She lifts a shoulder. "I don't know what I plan to do, but I really just don't have the desire to put my nose to the grindstone in a way that I know something like that would require. The thought of dealing with social media and customer service really exhausts me. I'm not even certain I have the mental capacity for it now. Would it upset you if I didn't?"

I take her hand on the table. I can't quite seem to stop touching her now. My heart gives a hopeful squeeze when she turns hers over to link her fingers with mine. "I'll support you no matter what you do. I mean that. I always have."

Her eyes meet mine, and she doesn't look away. "I'm starting to believe you."

Warmth spears through me. Tana must recognize it in my gaze because her lips part and her chest flushes with heat. Then the waitress stops by with an old-fashioned for me and a mojito for Tana. We both drink deeply, although the bourbon does nothing to cool the surge of lust.

"Thank you for dinner. It was wonderful."

I pull to a stop in the driveway and turn to her. Goddamn, but she's beautiful. "You're welcome."

A breath shudders past her lips. "What now?"

"What do you mean?"

"Where do we go from here?"

I take her hand in mine and bring it to my lips. "We go wherever you want to go."

"I don't want to hurt you," she says.

"You let me worry about that. I'm a big boy; I can take care of my feelings. I've told you before that nothing has changed. I'm here for you, no matter what."

"Because you're committed to your wife."

"Yes, that was why at first."

Her eyes snap to mine. "What do you mean?"

"I mean, a part of me will always love who you used to be. But that doesn't mean there isn't room for who you are now. I've got plenty of love for you to go around."

Tears shine in Tana's eyes. "But I feel like a completely different person. I don't want to wear the kind of clothes she wore. I don't want to be a social media influencer or even care about fashion. I like yoga pants and T-shirts and working in the garden and helping Penny at the rescue. I'd rather dig in the dirt in the garden than get my nails done."

"Yeah, what's your point?"

"My point is, how can you love *me* if I'm nothing like *her?*"

"Because you are the one who took care of my babies when they were sick even though I know you would have rather been anywhere else. You're the one who rescued a disabled stray cat instead of looking the other way. You're the one who moans my name like I've given you the best orgasm of your life. You don't have to be the woman you used to be for me to love you. I love you for *you.*"

I didn't mean to say the words so soon, didn't mean to play that card before she was ready, but there's no taking them back. They're true. At some point, my love for who she was and who she is now blurred. Now I can't imagine living without this woman—in all her versions. Always.

"Alec," she says through her tears.

I kiss the salt from her cheeks. "You don't have to say it back now. Not until you're ready. I've got all the time in the world to hear those words from you. All I ask is that when you say it, you don't ever stop."

She clears her throat and then nods. "Okay."

"Okay. You gonna kiss me now, or do I have to beg?"

Laughing, she leans over the center console and kisses me. When she doesn't pull away immediately, I deepen the kiss, parting her lips with my tongue and sinking my hands into her hair. I can't get enough of tasting her. . . everywhere. When we part, she's panting, her eyes are dilated, and her fingers grip my shirt collar.

"Can we go inside?" she asks.

I press my forehead against hers and try to get a handle on my impulses. "Sure. We can watch one of your true crime shows or something."

She reaches up and touches my lips, then meets my eyes. "I don't want to watch TV, Alec."

It doesn't take much to deduce what she wants instead. Groaning, I pull my hands back because I know if I keep touching her, I won't be able to stop. "Hang on, I'll get your door."

I move before she can say anything and round the truck to open her door and help her down. She's not fooled one bit. "Really?" Tana asks with a raised brow. "Do I need to get you drunk to put your hands on me again?"

The keys nearly slip to the concrete at my feet. "Tana. . ." I warn because my throat seizes. I move into the house and head to the kitchen, but I freeze when I see the kitchen island where I had her spread out in front of me, all pretty and pink.

I turn to move somewhere else, but she's blocking my path. Gulping for air, my back hits the wall. Cornered. By a woman six inches shorter than me and probably half my weight. But I'm trying to be a good man for her, give her time and space. I've pushed her enough.

"What are you afraid of?" she asks and moves closer to me. "Don't you want to kiss me again?"

I put my hands on her arms to stop her from moving closer. "Fuck, of course I do. But I want to do all the other things for you first. Take you out. Get to know you more. Give you time to get to know yourself and what you really want from life. You deserve to have so much, Tana, and I want to make sure you have everything."

She cups my cheek with a hand, her eyes staring deep into mine. "There's nothing you have to do to deserve me. I want you for who you are. Now take me to our bed, Alec. Please."

I fight an internal battle for all of ten seconds—the longest ten seconds of my life—and then break underneath her heated gaze. I scoop her up into my arms with a groan, her surprised shriek ringing in my ears as I throw her over my shoulder in a fireman's carry. With a firm smack on her ass, I say, "This is for ordering me around, woman."

She shrieks again, but this time it's punctuated with her

laughter. "How do you know I don't like it? What if I keep doing things because I want you to spank me more?"

I reach our bedroom and toss her onto the bed, where she lands in a sexy as hell sprawl, a feast in front of me. Something inside me unclenches at the sight of her back where she belongs. I know without a doubt this is where she'll be spending every night from here on out if I have a say in the matter.

"Don't tease me, or I'll have to redden that ass of yours to prove a point."

She doesn't even flinch. "Really?" In fact, if I'm not mistaken, the tone in her voice is excitement.

Groaning, I unbuckle my belt and set it down next to her on the bed. "You're killing me, girl. I'm trying to be sweet with you for your first time."

She rolls her eyes. "This isn't my first time."

"May as well be. Don't you want it to be perfect?" I climb into bed beside her and stretch out. There's no way in hell I'm going to rush this.

Tana unbuttons my shirt, her fingers tickling down my chest. By the time she reaches the bottom, my skin is on fire. When her eyes meet mine, so steady and sure, I'm trembling like it's my first time instead of hers.

"It's perfect because it's with you," she says, her voice breathy. Leaning forward, she presses her lips to the base of my throat. I shiver, full-body, and try to move away. "Don't. Let me touch you."

I roll to my back and put my hands behind my head. "All yours, sweet pea. Show me what you want."

She pushes up on one hand. "Really?" Nibbling on her lower lip, she admits, "I don't know where to start." The contradiction of shyness and desire is driving me crazy. It fucks with my mind a little because Tana had been aggressive as hell before the accident, always the initiator and very upfront about what she wanted. Don't get me wrong. It was hot as hell, and I always loved that she had no problem showing me she wanted me. But damn if I don't love having to coax it out of her now, too.

If nothing else, the accident has shown me all the different ways I can love my wife. If it all works out, I'll have a lifetime to discover a thousand more.

I work around the lump in my throat. "Tell me all the places you want to start, and I'll help you out."

Her lips twist. "Sounds like you're getting the short end of the stick."

"That's for later, darlin'. And there's nothing short about my stick."

Laughing, she sits up on her knees by my side, dips a finger under my shirt, and says, "Take your shirt off first. Let me get a better look at you."

I shrug out of my shirt and lay back on the bed. She sucks a lip between her teeth and lays a hand on my lower stomach, making the muscles twitch. Fire spreads from her fingertips. "This what you want?" I ask.

She watches her hands spread over my stomach and chest, and I realize my mistake. I'm going to die before she's done. Her fingertips trace the lines of my abs, up to my chest, circle around my nipples, and drag down my shoulders and arms. She reverses direction, her hands ending at the waistband of my jeans. Without answering my questions, she says, "Pants now."

"Go for it," I choke out. Pretty sure my hands would be shaking so much that I wouldn't be able to undo a fucking button.

She worries that lip between her teeth again as she undoes the button and zipper. I lift my hips as she pulls my jeans down my thighs. My briefs are melded to every inch of me, so I may as well be spread out naked in front of her. I don't think I've ever been so fucking happy in my life.

"What are you smiling for?" she asks, sitting back on her heels.

I reach up and palm her neck, wanting to bring her close to me, touch her everywhere, but I know I need to let her go at her own pace. "Didn't think I'd ever get to do this again. Have you back in my bed. Got a lot to smile for right now. Especially with your hands on me."

"It's not weird for you?" she asks and pulls back, putting her hands in her lap.

"Nothing with you could ever feel weird or wrong, sweet pea," I say and bring a hand to my lips, pressing a kiss to her palm. "Now come here and kiss me again. I want that mouth."

The leash she's had on her self-control snaps. She dives for me, and we tangle, lips and limbs.

Everything.

CHAPTER 19
TANA

I press my body against Alec's as he wraps his big arms around me, twisting until I'm underneath him. I barely notice because it positions his hips between my thighs, and my whole being focuses on the places we touch. Maybe it's muscle memory; maybe it's pure primal lust. Whatever the reason, it's instinctual how I respond to him when he touches me. My legs immediately wrap around his waist and my arms around his shoulders. No hesitation. Not anymore. I may only be certain about one thing in my life now, and it's him.

His heavy weight settles over me, grounding me and pinning me to the bed. The rock-hard body I've been admiring when I thought no one was looking is now all mine to explore, to enjoy, and I plan to make the most of every second. As he kisses me deeply, I map his strong back with my hands, something I've been dying to do for a while—even if I hadn't admitted it to myself before now. If I had to choose a favorite part of Alec, this would be a contender. It's strong and wide, expertly hewn with hard muscle, and smooth under my touch. I'm sure a lot of women would go for his equally lickable abs and Adonis belt, but there's something about the way his wide shoulders taper to his waist that really does it for me.

I'm so in his thrall that when he begins to rock his hips to grind against me, I moan so loud it shocks me a little. His briefs and the thin excuse for silk underwear I have underneath my dress are the only material separating us. We may as well be naked. I can feel every glorious inch of him.

Alec works the thick, hard ridge of his cock against my throbbing, needy center. I could come from this alone, I realize. I break the kiss and throw my head back, needing to breathe, but the air around us has grown thick and hot. I pull in deep inhales but can't seem to catch my breath.

Undeterred, Alec skims his lips along the line of my throat, biting down on the tender skin just under my jaw. I want to draw it out and explore the rest of his body with as much patience as I did his chest, but the desire inside me is racing to a fever pitch. When I can focus long enough, I tear my dress off and throw it blindly somewhere in the direction of the dresser. Alec gives me enough space to unhook the matching black bra, and it follows in the same direction as the dress.

Even though he's undoubtedly seen me naked countless times, his eyes feast on my bared breasts like it's the first time he's seen them. His head dips down, and his lips find a pebbled nipple with unerring precision. He sucks it deep into his mouth and alternates between licking the sensitive tip and sucking hard. I cry out in surprise and delight, rocking my hips against his hard cock, straining to get as close to him as possible.

"Please, Alec. I need you." The words sound like they're coming from another woman's mouth, but it's my own voice I'm hearing. Needy. Desperate. Dare I even say sexy?

Alec glances up at me. He has one hand cupping my breast for his pleasure, the pink nipple glistening, wet, and visible in what little light there is in the room. Pinching it between his fingers, he rolls it gently but hard enough that I feel the answering thrum in my lower belly. "Does that sweet pussy need me?" he asks as his fingers replace his lips.

My cheeks flush. The way he talks makes me want to do crazy, wild things. It makes me proud I can make such a wholesome, kind man so filthy. The words are stuck in my throat, so I can only nod down at him.

One of his hands goes to the waistband of my panties. He traces the edge with a fingertip and then molds his hand over the damp center, the heat blistering me from the inside out. I throw my head against the pillow and thrash from side to side. He seems determined to tease me into insanity even though I'm the one who started this.

"Not gonna do anything until you answer me. Tell me what you want."

"You." There. That's honest. I can't think of anything else I want more at this moment.

He pushes aside the fabric and bares me to his searing gaze. "Oh, baby, you are wet for me, aren't you? I bet this needy little pussy would swallow me right up. Tell me how much you want it," he demands.

"I want it," I repeat. "I want it so much. Please give it to me." I am mindless at this point. I'd give him anything he wanted. Tell him anything he wants.

"What do you want? Be specific." He drops down to a forearm, his free hand teasing my swollen, throbbing clit.

The desperate emptiness inside me has me begging, "Fill me up, please. I want you inside me." I should be shocked to hear those words coming from my mouth, but his naked dirty talk is apparently contagious.

His answering hedonistic grin is consolation enough. And then he says, "That's a good girl. That's my good fucking girl." And all shame is gone. I like knowing that I can turn him on just as much as he does me. Not a random woman, not a stranger. Not even the woman who used to be his wife. He wants me, for me. That's all I've ever needed to know.

Without pause, he pulls my panties down my legs and shocks the hell out of me when he presses them to his nose, inhaling deeply. Oh god. That shouldn't be as hot as it is, but the look on his face has me writhing under him.

He hovers over me and whispers, "You smell so fucking good. Open your mouth."

I do as he says because it turns me on to do things he likes. He balls up the panties and puts them in my mouth. The scent of me fills my nose, and it's a heady, drugging thing.

"I want you to taste how much you want me when I am inside you," he murmurs.

Unable to speak, all I can do is nod and watch as he strips off his briefs, giving me the barest glimpse of his cock. It's only enough for me to realize that there's no way that thing will fit. I'm both eager to have him inside me and a little uneasy about how he'll get there.

As though he can read my mind—or perhaps he sees how wide my eyes have gotten—he produces a bottle of lube and lays it next to me on the bed. "Don't worry, baby. I'll take care of you." Still a little hesitant, I shift, unable to talk because my mouth is full. His smile spreads slowly, wickedly, and if I could frown at him, I would. Maybe there's a bit of a sadist in him because I think he's enjoying this. "You can take it all."

I shake my head from side to side because part of me doesn't quite believe him. He looks like he could split me wide open.

He leans forward to kiss my forehead. "If you want to stop, you can take those out at any time, okay?"

I nod because I'm curious to see how he thinks he's going to manage this and because I want him so badly now it hurts.

He tests my wetness with two thick fingers, thrusting them deep inside me. I moan, forgetting about my nerves and apprehension. I sob for air around the fabric of my panties and palm my breasts, scissoring the sensitive tips between my fingers. Alec notices and teases my clit with an expert thumb. "That's my fucking girl. Show me what feels good. Get yourself ready for me."

As I pinch and squeeze my nipples, he wets the head of his dick at the entrance to my pussy. He won't even need any lube; that's how wet I am. I'm trembling all over with antici-pation. Maybe some apprehension. That sharp bite of some-thing akin to fear has me practically dripping.

One big, tanned hand holds my thighs spread wide while the other guides the head of his cock inside in one gentle push. I wiggle my hips and bite down on the material in my mouth to bear it.

"That's it, baby. You can take it. You can take all I've got to give you, can't you?"

I'm not sure I can, but I love it when he praises me, so I nod wildly. He thrusts again, forcing another inch inside me. The sensation of stretching around him consumes me. My eyes flutter closed, and he thrusts again, and *finally*, his thick cock is fully inside. He fills me to the point of delicious pain, but it hurts so good all I can do is gasp around the panties in my mouth.

He shoves my thighs up and wide to circle his waist, opening me to every hard, unrepentant thrust. I lose the capacity for coherent speech as his cock hits deep with preci-sion. The friction of his girth, steady, consuming pace, and the knowledge that he's mine, all mine if I'll have him, has me clenching around him. The orgasm seizes me in a vicious tangle, exploding behind my now closed eyelids and spreading throughout my body.

Because he's not only mine, now.

I'm his.

CHAPTER 20
ALEC

"How weird is it to be with her?" Jax asks, lifting a half-empty beer to his lips. Walker elbows him in the ribs, but Jax persists. "No, really. Is it like being with a stranger? Or like being with your wife like normal? It's gotta be freaky, dude. In more ways than one."

I roll my eyes at Jax, not rising to his taunts. As the rookie of the group and the resident playboy, Jax is *always* the one with the snarky ass comment. "Not as weird as half the shit you're into, I'm sure," I say, leveling him with a look. "It's a birthday party, dude. Try to keep it PG." I glance at Walker, who grins back and helps redirect Jax to the refreshments table.

Shaking my head, I return to the grill I'm manning and dutifully flip hotdogs and hamburgers. Around me, a gaggle of neighborhood kids and the girls' classmates screech and dart from the gigantic bounce house to a collection of sprinklers and water toys. A rainbow of balloons dances in the background, several already deflating in the Florida heat. The scent of grass, sizzling meat, and sweaty kids hangs in the air.

Tana flits from the table to the kitchen and back again, her face flushed from too much sun and exertion. I'm not entirely sure when she got up this morning, but my internal alarm woke me up at six. She already had two trays of cupcakes cooling on the counter. The whole interior was decorated with balloons, streamers, confetti, and God only knows what else. By the time our driveway began filling with cars, she'd also hung dangling lights, arranged tables in the backyard for presents, prepared a veritable feast of every dessert imaginable, and still looked sweet as hell in a summer sundress that swished around her tantalizing legs.

I curse as the hot dogs begin to burn and quickly remove them to a serving tray before they're completely charred. Kids are screaming, the backyard will be a disaster zone, and the girls will probably be up for the next month based on the amount of sugar they've consumed alone, but damn if I'm not content for the first time in what feels like weeks.

"What are you smiling for?" Remy asks as he divests himself of an outrageously sized birthday gift bag. He grabs a beer from the adult section of the beverage station, pops the top, and drinks deeply.

"Got a lot to be thankful for today, man. Glad you could make it."

"Well, little squirt made me promise I'd come and give her shooting lessons."

I glance up from the grill. "Don't tell me that's a gun in there, man."

At this, Remy cracks an uncharacteristic smile. "Fine, I won't tell you."

"Jesus Christ, Rem."

"It's just a BB gun. She can't do much damage with it yet. Didn't you get one when you turned ten or eleven too?"

I hold my tongue because if Tana hears me say something about gender, I know I'll get a lecture about women being as capable as men—that at least hadn't changed after the accident.

"Whatever, just keep it away from her until all these potential victims leave the scene."

We fall into a comfortable silence for a while, only punctuated by the sound of the doorbell ringing occasionally and doors slamming. Remy sticks to the corner near the grill, a shoulder leaning against the deck railing, observing the going's on without joining.

"You hear Lettie's back?" he asks without looking at me.

I glance up sharply. "You're shitting me," I say, dumbstruck.

"No less than five people stopped me on the way here from the front yard to tell me."

"She here to see her mom?" I let the question hang off. From the stiff set of his shoulders, I deduce Lettie Samuels didn't return to Battleboro for a friendly visit.

Remy's frown deepens. "She's moving back. Been here a couple weeks. I guess making it big on Broadway didn't work out for her."

In a town like Battleboro, Colette Samuels, former Miss Florida returning with her tail between her legs, may have been front-page news. The fact that she and Remy got along like oil and water explains why Remy looks like he swallowed a porcupine.

"That's crazy," I say as I plate up the rest of the hamburgers. Tana comes to take them from me and gives me a heated look over the trays.

"It is what it is," Remy says and lifts a shoulder. "As long as she sticks to her side of town and me to mine, we won't have a problem."

I seriously doubted that. Years ago, Remy's dad married Lettie's mother. Lettie and Remy fought more often than not, and it was a coin toss as to who was the bigger bully. Remy may be the size of a tanker and intimidating, but Lettie is half Italian and hot-headed to boot. They spent part of the time living together in vicious confrontations and the rest trying not to tear each other's clothes off. During Lettie's senior year of high school, everything came to a head when their house caught fire. Lettie made it out. Remy's dad didn't.

Things between them were never the same, and Remy never forgave her.

"I'm sure she's changed."

"It doesn't fucking matter. She'll steer clear of me if she knows what's good for her."

"Excuse me," Tana says, worry knitting her brow. "Have you seen Paisley anywhere? I can't find her, and it's time to eat. Can you help me look?"

Remy nods to me. "You go. I'll clean up around here."

"Thanks." To Tana, I say, "She has to be around here

somewhere. There's no way that girl would miss out on food."

"Of course," Tana answers, but her frown is pronounced, and there's sweat on her brow. The first ribbons of unease tangle in my stomach.

We look in the bounce house first but only find Gemma and a couple of their friends. With a quick word to my mom to keep an eye on Gemma, we go through the house room by room, calling Paisley's name. But she's not in any of them.

"When's the last time you saw her?" I ask Tana when we've exhausted all the rooms in the house. I shove a hand through my hair and spin in a tight circle. There's no one around but a couple parents sneaking foul-smelling cigarettes in the front yard. The excited shrieks from the children in the backyard sound light-years away, and the blistering summer sun bakes my skin, making me feel itchy and tight all over.

"I swear she was just here. I thought she went inside to go to the bathroom." Tana's voice is frantic, and she twists her hands together. She's trying to stay calm and composed, but her mouth quivers.

"She has to be here somewhere," I say, more to reassure myself. "Let's split up. She can't have gone far."

Several other parents have noticed the unease in the air. I hear a couple of them dividing up, some to stay with the kids and distribute hot dogs and hamburgers to keep them distracted, and the others peel off in cars to cruise the nearby streets. I see Jax, Walker, Zeke, and Remy take to the sidewalk to go door to door, but I can't make myself move for fear that she'll come back and I won't be here when she does.

Please be okay.

The thought of losing someone else. . . it's unfathomable. I only just got Tana back. Losing one of my girls. . . I can't even contemplate it.

"Daddy?" comes Gemma's voice. "Daddy, what's wrong? Where's Paisley?"

I turn to find Gemma in her Little Mermaid swimsuit, red faced and sweaty from the sun. She's holding a juice in one hand and a balloon on a string in another. I choke back a sob and get on my knees in front of her. "She'll be right back. Why don't you go and get some cake while we wait?"

Gemma, who normally won't turn down a dessert, frowns at me. "But we didn't sing Happy Birthday to her."

"It's okay. She won't mind if you have some."

"No, I'm not having cake without Paisley." A tired whine colors her voice. "Tell her to hurry up."

"Okay, baby, okay. Go to the backyard and wait for her. I'll tell her to hurry up." She hesitates for a moment and then does what I say.

My head droops, and I order myself to pull it together. Shoving to my feet, I grit my teeth and try to think. Paisley may be stubborn and emotional, but she would never wander off, especially not during her birthday. Not without good reason after what happened to Tana. There has to be something I'm missing.

It's then I hear her raised voice. My heart clenches in relief, but she isn't shouting with joy. She's screaming.

I bolt toward her shouts, flying past Jax and Walker. I

ignore Tana's concerned face and vault over a locked fence gate.

"This is his fault! If it weren't for him, I'd still have my mother!"

The words don't make sense until I round the corner of the brick house, veering around a broken-down lawn mower and wading through knee-high grass to find Paisley being held back by Angela. Leon cowers in front of her, stone-faced and shirtless, his shoulders blistering in the sun.

"If you weren't a bunch of drunks, your son wouldn't have hit my mom and killed her. She's dead! If you were a better father, I'd still have a mom, and your son would still be alive!" I hear my words regurgitate from her tight lips, and my stomach rolls.

Paisley is a torrent of rage. Her translucent skin is reddened with anger, and her pretty curls are falling out of the elaborate updo she begged for this morning. Her bathing suit cover-up is dangling off one shoulder, and she's not wearing any shoes, but she doesn't seem to notice.

"Paisley," I grind out. She doesn't seem to hear me at first. She finally turns to me, tears streaming down her freckled cheeks, when I put a hand on her thin, shaking shoulder. "Paisley, honey."

She throws herself at my side, her body wracked with sobs. "It's his fault. It is! If he wasn't such a bad dad, his son wouldn't have been drinking and driving." She gasps through a violent bout of hiccups. "He wouldn't have hit Mom, and she would still be here, and I wouldn't feel so alone all the time."

If she'd shoved me into a speeding semi, I would have been less stunned. "Paisley," I croak out.

"I think you should go," his daughter says quietly.

Knowing I need to remove Paisley from this shitshow, I pull her up into my arms and turn my back on them. I'll deal with them later. The first thing I see is Tana's stricken expression.

Fuck.

"I want to go home," Paisley says through her tears.

I send Tana a begging look, and she quietly steps out of my way so we can move by.

Within twenty minutes, the birthday party is shut down. Most of the cars are gone, and all that's left are the garbage bags full of used plates and sticky cups, drunkenly hanging streamers, and stacks of unopened presents piled in the laundry room. Mom distracted Gemma in the backyard with water balloons, bless her.

The moment we got home, Paisley ripped herself from my arms, ran to her room, and slammed the door behind her. She's been here ever since. I wanted to give her time to cool down, so I let her be until everyone else left.

When the door closes behind the last person, I turn and rest against it. Pulling my phone from my back pocket, I call the girls' therapist's emergency line and request an appointment as soon as possible. I'm doing my best to help them navigate everything, but let's be honest, we all need professional help sometimes. And I'm pretty certain this situation warrants professional help. Because God knows I don't know what the fuck I'm doing.

Tana is waiting in the kitchen, washing the same spot on the kitchen counter she's been washing since the last time I checked on her.

"How is she?" Tana asks, clutching and twisting the dishrag in both hands.

"I'm about to go check on her. How are you?"

She gnaws on her lip and then says, "I'm alright. I think it's probably best if I give you two a little time. I've already called Penny. The one who helped me with the cat. She's going to let me stay at her place for a few days. Give Paisley some space to breathe."

"Tana," my voice goes out. I clear my throat and try again. "You don't have to do that. Stay. Everything will be fine."

She shakes her head, and I can tell by the stubborn set of her chin that she's already made up her mind. "I've been so focused on me I didn't even think of these girls, Alec. They're what's important here. You know that. Paisley has had problems from the beginning. She needs you now, I think."

The radio squawks, and my phone alert goes off at the same time. "Attention. I need you to respond to First Baptist on Second Street for a structure fire."

Tana's face goes blank, and I grit my teeth before picking up the radio to respond to the call. "This is Battleboro 8. I'll be en route with Tanker 2." The last thing I want to do is leave Tana now with everything feeling unresolved, but we live the closest to the church, and if the feeling in my gut is any indication, it may be the second arson case our small town has ever seen. "I've gotta go, but I want you here when I get back."

"Go. We'll work everything out later. I'll have your mom stay with the girls."

"Just. . ." I shove a hand through my hair. "Don't make any rash decisions. Stay with Penny if you need to, but let me deal with Paisley and work this out. Please."

"You should go," she says.

"I'll come for you when I'm done with this, and the girls are okay."

She doesn't say anything, but she hugs me fiercely. It'll have to be enough for now.

CHAPTER 21
ALEC

I turn it off while I retrieve my gear and speed over to the church. There's nothing else I can do but my job. When I arrive at the address, smoke billows out, sooty black against the clear, blue sky. Flames lick from openings in the structure, waves of heat emanate from the rippling sheets of fire, and ash rains down like soft snow. Familiar faces watch, awestruck, as ropes of fire destroy everything in its path.

First Baptist has sat empty since the hurricane, the structural damage too severe for repair. The new church was built closer to the elementary school. Unfortunately, there are a lot of dilapidated properties like this around Lake County turning to ruins of their former selves. It's no surprise that all I can do is control the fire until it spends itself out. It was a tinder box in such recent dry weather.

Zeke arrives at the scene, grim-faced underneath his gear. For once, I'm glad I'm not the one in charge. I'd hate to deal with the investigation, the spotlight, and the blowback from the town when this is confirmed as arson, too. Tension is already high after no new leads on the gym fire.

It doesn't make any sense. Battleboro has barely three thousand residents. Most people here grew up together, work together, and our kids are friends. I can't imagine anyone we know being responsible for something like this. It feels hateful, personal. Like someone is attacking the heart of Battleboro by destroying pieces of its history.

An hour later, most of the fire is contained. What's left of the church is now a mass of blackened wood, shattered glass, and other unidentifiable debris. The crowd watching has doubled in size, and there is an identical expression on all their faces: disbelief.

"I'll take over here," Zeke says. "I know you've got a lot to deal with back home. Remy and Walker are on the way."

For the first time in my career, I leave the scene at his request and go home. There's no way I'm making the same mistake twice, knowing I should be home with my family when they need me. Mom's car is in the driveway when I pull up. The remnants of the party still litter the sidewalk. Hard to think that had only happened a few hours ago. It feels like years.

Gemma and Mom are passed out on the couch. I find Paisley in her room, looking so small and innocent in her pastel sheets and quilt. She starts in surprise when I step in, and she rolls over in bed, sniffling and rubbing her face. My heart breaks into a thousand pieces because I know this is one of those things I simply can't fix for her, and I hate that.

"Paise, baby. We need to talk." I close the door so we don't wake Gemma or my mom. There's an ache in my belly driving me to look for Tana and make certain she didn't run, but Paisley needs me, too.

"I don't—don't want to," she hiccups. "I want you to leave me alone."

"I can't do that, sweetheart, and you know it. We have to talk about what happened."

Her little shoulders shake with the effort of her tears. God, I fucking hate this. "You're going to tell me I have to apologize to Mr. Leon, but I won't. I meant every word. If it wasn't for him and his son, Mom would be okay. She would have remembered I liked strawberry cake, not chocolate. She wouldn't have needed to be reminded today was my birthday." She takes a good few minutes to get all the words out between her tears. With each one, my heart cracks a little more.

Stretching out on the bed behind her, I wrap my arms around her. I'd give anything to take away this pain. If I could protect her and Gemma from this, I would do whatever it required in a heartbeat. One of the worst things about being a parent is when you know your kids have realized you're infallible. "I know, honey. I wish those things too, sometimes."

There's a pause, punctuated with a sniffle. "You do?"

"Of course I do. I miss her too, very much. It's okay to be sad about it, even mad sometimes. I'll never get onto you about that. It's been very hard on all of us, and you've been so brave and so strong for your sister. But it's okay for you to not be okay."

"I thought—thought I'd be okay when she came home because at least she didn't die, but this is almost worse." She shudders with her tears. "It's like living with her ghost."

"Oh, honey." I give in and scoop her up from the covers to hold her little body in my lap. She cries into my chest, something she hasn't really done since the accident. "I know it's hard. It's been hard on me, too. On everyone." Rubbing her back gently, I kiss her hair. "But it's not okay to bottle these feelings up. That's what we have Dr. Teatree for. To tell him how we're feeling so we can figure out how to deal with it as a family. So we don't go yelling at our neighbors."

"He deserved it."

Sighing, I say, "Can't say I haven't wanted to do a little hollering myself, and sometimes you're entitled. But if you hold on to that kind of anger, it festers inside of you until you're angry all the time. And that's not the kind of life you want to live, sweet girl. It's my job as your dad to help you deal with it and give you the tools to express it in a healthy way. But it's your job to tell me when you need help."

"I didn't want to make you upset when you seemed so happy to have her home."

I close my eyes and press my cheek against her head. When did she get so damn grown-up? "You don't worry about that. I'm responsible for my own feelings, too, but yours come first."

All the tension melts out of her, and she breathes deeply. "Dad?" Paisley asks.

"Yeah, sweetheart?"

"Do you think there's any cake left?"

Chuckling, I help her to her feet. "I'm sure we can find some."

We find plenty of cake and ice cream. What—or should I say who—I don't find is Tana. Not that I'm truly surprised.

Mom eyes me like she wants to tell me to go the hell after her, but she wisely holds her tongue. After she leaves, I clean up the rest of the mess from the birthday party, feeling hollow and spent. I'm fighting every urge inside me to go after her, but my instincts tell me she needs time.

So, I'll give her time.

And then I'm going after what's mine.

What's always been mine.

CHAPTER 22

TANA

"This is Reduced Fat Sour Cream," Penny says with a bright smile. "Don't mind him. He's very friendly, despite his appearance." She indicates a cat of epic proportions perched on her guest bed like an ancient miniature lion. And it wouldn't be wrong because, good God, that's the biggest cat I've ever seen. He's got a larger than average head and a massive bulky body with fur the color of toasted cream. "I call him Creamy. Dreamy Creamy. Mr. Cream Puff. He won't bother you unless you don't like snuggles. If that's the case, I'll put him in my room. Better yet, why don't I do that now?" Penny rambles. She tugs at her wild brown waves and gives me a nervous but friendly smile.

"No, I don't mind at all. I could use the company." I take a seat on the bed next to the big cat, who immediately ambles over to me and purrs. Sifting my hands through his soft fur, I try not to think about the cat I left at Alec's. I miss her already. "Thank you again for letting me stay here. I really appreciate it."

"Don't sweat it! No one uses this room except my mom when she visits a couple of times a year. It mostly belongs to Creamy and the occasional foster cat. Or raccoon. Or squirrel. You get the idea."

"How long have you worked at the rescue?" I ask.

Her pixie-cute face screws up with concentration. "Oh, going on five years now, I guess. I started volunteering there during college. Then I guess I never left. Once I got my degree, I sort of just took over for Mrs. Bixby, the lady who ran it initially. I've always loved animals, and it drove my parents crazy that I would always bring home strays, but I could never turn down an animal in need. They wanted me to be a *people* doctor," she adds with disgust.

"I can't picture you as a people doctor," I say.

She gestures wildly. "Right? But tell them that. Thankfully they moved to California a while ago, so I don't have to listen to that constantly." Penny is a ball of wild energy. I don't think she's stopped moving since I showed up on her front doorstep. She paces from bookshelf to dresser to desk, touching keepsakes, rearranging books, and picking at chipping paint.

Creamy settles onto my lap, a big overflowing cat loaf. I'm grateful for both him and the conversation to distract me from how utterly miserable I feel. "So you grew up here in Battleboro, too?"

Penny smiles a huge, friendly grin. "Uh-huh! I was a couple years behind you and Alec, though. And I was a year behind Jax—the guy who works with Alec. Anyway, we've been best friends for years, although I've had a schoolgirl crush on him for most of my life, not that he's noticed."

"He's the younger one, right?" Keeping all the names and faces straight has been a challenge, but it's starting to get easier with practice and time. That's promising, at least. Maybe my memory—or lack thereof—won't always be the obstacle that it is now.

"The rookie, yeah. Totally gorg, right? Alas, I don't think he'll ever see me as anything other than his kid sister." She makes a face and shakes it off. "Story of my life. No one really takes me seriously. I'm pretty sure he still sees me as the knobby twelve-year-old with braces and a lisp."

I give her a once-over while shaking my head. Penny is a knockout in a girl next door sort of way. Wavy brown hair the color of pine bark, soft, kind green eyes, and an energetic, friendly nature you can't help but feel endeared to. "Is he *blind*?" I ask emphatically, causing Creamy to jump and stretch a little at the increase in volume.

Penny gives a warm, full laugh. "He's a man. So naturally, he can't see what's right in front of him."

"I don't know him well, or you know *at all*, but I think he'd have to be crazy not to be completely in love with you."

"That's what I'm screamin'!" she says. Then she does a little hop and claps her hands. "You know what we need to forget all our troubles?"

"Wine?" I think of how my last foray with alcohol went and feel dubious.

"Something even better!"

"Is there anything—"

"Kittens!" she exclaims.

Ten minutes later, we're sitting on the floor of her spare bathroom with a pile of kittens in our laps. "Okay, yeah," I say with a laugh. "This is so much better than wine."

"Gemma has a game today. She'd like you to come."

I close my eyes against the yearning that squeezes around my heart when I hear Alec's voice. It's been less than a week, and already I miss him and the girls so much it nearly hurts. I don't know if it's because I've grown to care for them in such a short time or because part of me already knows them, loves them, and feels their absence so intensely. Either way, I think about them pretty much constantly.

"Are you sure that's a good idea?" I gnaw on my thumbnail. "I thought we'd decided after your conversation with Paisley that we should give them some space."

"We did. I think it's been space enough."

Side-stepping the question, I say, "What did their therapist say?"

"Dr. Teatree said it's natural for there to be an adjustment period. It's going to be hard for the girls for a long time, but we need to be consistent for them. The last thing they need is more upheaval."

Penny steps into the doorway and pauses when she finds me on the phone. I make a "one-minute" gesture, and she gives me a thumbs up. "Doesn't that mean we should give them time to adjust? Maybe we should take this even slower for them. Give everyone time to process that this is the right thing."

"Having our family together is the right thing." He pauses for a long time. "Unless that's not what you want."

"Of course it's what I want," I murmur, my heart squeezing.

"Then come to the game. We can start slow, but we want you there. Please."

I wage an internal battle for all of three seconds before I cave. Who am I kidding? I've missed them—missed him so damn much. "Okay, fine. What time and where?"

He tells me the location. "Five. I can pick you up."

"No, that's okay. I have to help Penny close up tonight. I'll have her drive me, and we can meet you there."

"See you then," he says.

"Bye, Alec," I whisper.

The conflict must be written on my face because Penny leans across the front counter. "That Alec?" she asks.

"Yeah. Do you mind driving me over to the rec field? Gemma has a game, and they want me to go."

"Hell yeah. I love me some concession stand food."

"Penny, you are one of a kind."

"Damn straight."

After spending the week working at the rescue with Penny, I officially know I won't ever go back to the business before-me used to own. I love working with the animals too much, and I have no desire to lead the face-paced lifestyle before-me had and run all those social media accounts, let alone make the clothes that were sold. I made the announcement a few days ago with a short life update video on the business's Instagram and YouTube. To say my followers were disappointed was an understatement, but most were pretty understanding, considering. The outpouring of kindness was unexpected and appreciated. But it was also like a weight lifted off my chest to make that distinction.

After-me likes my privacy and solitude. She likes kissing Alec and cooking with the girls. After-me likes going for long walks in the woods and binging true crime podcasts and documentaries. I plan to donate most of before-me's clothes, at least the ones I know I'll never wear, and keep the more casual stuff. While those clothes are nice and beautiful, I like being comfortable more.

My last checkup with Dr. Rennen cleared me of physical therapy. While he was disappointed my memories hadn't yet returned, he was pleased I hadn't had any further side effects so far and was confident my recall would only improve with time. As much as I wanted my memories to return, I'm not so certain now. I've finally come to terms with who I am now, and I'm happy with the direction my life is taking.

After my first few days at the rescue, I asked Penny if she needed any help. Though I didn't need the money, she accepted enthusiastically. The pay isn't anything special, but I love working with the animals, with my hands, and Penny is a riot. There hasn't been a dull day yet.

"Penny, why are you putting traps in your truck?" I ask after we finish closing up.

Penny pauses from loading the cages we use to trap stray and feral cats and winks. "Just in case."

"Are you expecting to run into a colony of feral cats?"

"It wouldn't be the first time."

"Of course not."

Penny's rental house, where she runs her rescue, is smack dab in the middle of one of the biggest feral cat colonies in Lake County. When she moved in, she set to work trapping, treating, and fixing all the cats she could. The ones she could tame got adopted out, and she kept a watchful eye on the others. Her family and friends may think she's flighty and eccentric, but I don't see how. I've only known her for a short while, and she's the most dedicated, passionate person I've ever met.

The recreation field is packed with cars when we arrive a short while later. Penny fights off a mom in a Karen haircut for a parking spot nearest the softball fields and cackles with glee as she puts her truck in park. Nerves jangle anew in my stomach at the prospect of seeing Alec again in front of all these people. It occurs to me he may have some sort of big scene planned, like something jumbotron equivalent. But he wouldn't do that, would he? That's something before-me may have liked, but the last thing I want now is more attention.

We get a few side-eyes every now and then, and I touch

my bangs to make sure they're covering my scar. Then I realize it's because Penny is waving or talking to nearly every person we meet and not because of my scar. The tension in my stomach loosens a little.

The metal stands are packed with people at each field, and the colorful jerseys of parents supporting their kids dot the crowd in a kaleidoscope of color. Teens hawk treats and gear from the concession stand as Penny stops for a veritable feast of grease and sugar. With her goodies in tow, we find Gemma's game in progress at the field next to the concession stand.

"Do you see them?" I whisper to her anxiously.

"Not yet—oh! Yes! There they are right behind home plate. Excellent. We'll have a good view."

Shouts and screams break out among the spectators as a bat cracks against the ball. The parents of the batter jump to their feet and wave and clap as the little girl makes it safely to first base. Parents from the other team mutter and gesture, but the umpire waves the next batter to home plate.

But I don't notice any of it because I finally spot Alec. And it's like my body knows. My heart knows. I simply come to life at the mere sight of him. A fireworks show grand enough for the Fourth of July takes place in my stomach, zinging across my nerve endings and causing my heart to pound wildly in my chest and ears.

He's standing behind two chairs with his arms crossed over his chest as he studies the field. Paisley and Tracy are in front of him on the edge of their seats. All three of them have DORRAN and the number seven on the backs of their matching purple jerseys. It hits me like a foul ball to the head. I want this. I want to be a part of their team. I want the Meatball Mondays, the sick days, the late-night emergency calls, the stolen moments in the kitchen, and the chaotic birthdays. I want it with this man, and I want it with these girls.

But the question is: do they still want it with me?

CHAPTER 23
ALEC

"She's gonna choke," Paisley says around a sip of soda. "She always chokes."

"You mind your mouth now, Paisley Grace," Mom admonishes. "This is your sister's first year playing. We're here to support her."

"Support her when she chokes," Paisley says under her breath.

I put a hand on her shoulder, and her mouth snaps closed. I don't think Paisley will ever totally heal from Tana's accident—it's written in the fabric of her life now, part of her story. But I do know I'll be there with her every step of the way to make sure she knows she's not alone—that she'll never be alone.

"There she is," Mom says and sits up straighter in her chair. "Let's go, number seven! Knock it outta the park!"

This time, Paisley keeps her mouth shut. Progress.

"Alright, Gem!" I shout over the din of cheers, coaches, and chants from her team. "Keep your eye on the ball. If it's there, you hit it hard. You got this!"

She looks so small out there with the other girls. I want to run and put my arms around her, protect her and maybe hide her away so she won't ever face the possibility of messing up. But she'd probably hit me with the bat, so I hold my ground and my breath as the pitcher winds up. The first pitch comes in wild—a ball. I let out a breath. Goddamn, this has to be more stressful for me than it is for her.

The chants from the dugout increase in volume as the next pitch comes in—a strike. I suck in a breath and shout, "That's alright, honey. Next one is yours."

"Let's go, Gemma!" Mom shouts.

Paisley is sitting forward in her seat, her eyes unwavering from where her sister is crouched over home plate. When it comes down to it, Paisley would step in front of a bus for her sister—or in this case, a softball.

The next two pitches are wild again, and then she swings at one that's too low and misses. Full count. I really wish they let people drink at these things. It would help my damn nerves. I don't know what's worse—watching your kid potentially fail or facing that potential yourself. I haven't heard from Tana yet. I hope she's still coming.

"Full count," yells the umpire.

"You got it, Gem. Come on, girl!" I yell.

Gemma takes a steadying breath at the plate looking all too vulnerable. My shoulders are somewhere around my ears by the time the pitcher releases the ball. Gemma swings and connects, the ball driving toward shortstop. She stares uncomprehendingly until Paisley shouts, "GO! RUN Gemma, run!" Then she's off like a shot toward first. Shortstop misses the ball, but it's scooped up by left field, who chucks it at second to cut Gemma off. But it doesn't matter. Our girl is safe at first.

"Woooo! Yay, Gemma! You go, girl! Great job!"

The feminine shout has me spinning to my left, and I find Tana with her hands cupped around her mouth, bouncing on the balls of her feet. Her hair is up in a sloppy bun, she's covered in cat hair, and she doesn't have a lick of makeup on. And I don't think I've ever seen her look more beautiful.

"You came," I choke out. I guess a part of me hadn't been sure she would.

"She really got that one good," Tana says. "Wow, that's incredible."

I unstick my tongue from the roof of my mouth. "Yeah, uh, my captain Zeke's been practicing with her a little. He played pro ball a long time ago."

Paisley turns to say something to me and notices Tana. Her mouth falls open, and her eyes bug out. Tana freezes, probably afraid Paisley may have another outburst like the one at her party. But then Paisley is jumping to her feet, her chair falling over, and throwing herself bodily into Tana's arms. Tana gives a hiccuping cry of surprised delight, and her arms go around Paisley's shoulders. Beside them, Penny is jumping gleefully.

"I'm so sorry!" Paisley wails. "I didn't mean it. I don't want you to go again. I've missed you so much. I promise I'll do better. Just please come home."

Tana's shocked gaze meets mine. I smile gently at her and lift a shoulder. Such is the life surrounded by women. It's a chaotic tornado of emotional outbursts. But I wouldn't have it any other way.

"You don't have to do anything better," Tana says gently and kneels in front of Paisley. "You didn't do anything wrong —aside from not telling anyone where you were going. You should always let someone know where you'll be because you about gave your father and me a heart attack. And if he has a heart attack, we're in big trouble because I'm not the one who can bring people back to life."

"I promise it won't happen again," Paisley says tearfully.

"That's good." Tana pulls Paisley back into her arms, her eyes falling closed as they embrace. I don't know if she realizes that her body goes soft, curving around Paisley. Her expression does, too, like she's holding onto something she didn't know she was missing. "And you don't need to apologize. We're all doing the best we can. I don't blame you for having a hard time."

Paisley tightens her hold on Tana, and they sway there, holding each other for a long time. My heart swells looking at the two of them, and for the first time since the accident, it feels almost whole again. The only thing missing is Tana promising to be in my bed every night until they tear us out of it.

When Paisley finally lets go and straightens, wiping her

eyes, Gemma is on third base, having been walked through the next two batters. Mom herds Paisley back to her chair with a knowing wink in my direction.

I turn back to Tana with pleads, promises, and okay, a little begging on my lips, but she's throwing herself into my arms before I can utter a word. Her lips capture mine as she presses her body against me. My hands go around her waist to hold her up, and I swear I'm never going to let her go.

Somewhere in the distance, a cheer goes up over the crowd, followed by guffaws of laughter and shouts. Vaguely, I hear someone shouting Gemma's name, but it takes me a minute to pull myself away from the heaven of Tana's lips. When I manage to, I find Gemma's coaches yelling at her and Gemma running away from third, off the field, through the dugout, and around the bleachers. Her face is red underneath her helmet, and tears are streaming down her cheeks.

She sprints to us and throws herself into our embrace, and Tana is laughing, her arms squeezing tight around us. Then Mom and Paisley are slamming into us too until it's one big pile of women with me at the center.

And I wouldn't have it any other way.

Amidst it all, I say to Tana, "So does this mean you're coming home?"

She reaches up with her free hand and lays it on my cheek. "If you'll still have me."

I can't stop the responding grin. The relief I feel is overwhelming. I look at the girls who are clutching each other and smiling so big I'm pretty sure I can count all their teeth. "What do you say, girls?"

"YES!" they shout simultaneously.

Then, as the game continues around us and the girls start hugging and jumping up and down, I kiss Tana again, and it feels like the first time all over again.

⚒ 232 ⚒

EPILOGUE

ALEC

"Shh, be quiet. We can't let Dad hear," comes the stage whisper, which may as well be a shout.

"*Gemma*! If you don't want Dad to hear, then maybe you shouldn't scream like a banshee," comes Paisley's caustic retort. I snort under my breath.

"I'm not screaming," Gemma says petulantly.

"Alright, girls, you don't have to sneak in," Tana says, easily smoothing over the spat. "Your dad won't be upset."

At this, Paisley snorts, and it sounds so much like mine I muffle a laugh. "Yeah, right. He said if you brought home any more animals, he was going to make us sleep outside with them. He said we didn't have enough room for any more. Especially not wild ones."

"Darla isn't wild!" Gemma protests. "She's a lady. Aren't you Darla?" I don't know how to describe the answering animal noise, but it's not one I've ever heard come from a domesticated critter. I sigh, but it's a contented one. I'd let

Tana bring home two of every species on the planet if it's what would make her happy, but I sure as hell don't tell them that.

"We should have snuck it around the side gate," Paisley says instead of answering her sister. "That way, we could have put it in a pen. Dad would never notice with all the other animals we have out there."

I can hear the restrained laughter in Tana's voice all the way from the bedroom. "I think the only reason he lets us have so many animals now is that we don't keep them a secret from him."

"You may be okay sleeping outside with them," Paisley replies without missing a beat, "but I like my bed. I don't want to sleep with a bunch of rabbits and chickens. I'm telling you, we should have snuck it in. He wouldn't notice."

"Paisley Grace, you better not be sneaking anything around this house," I say, finding the three of them huddled over an animal-carrying cage at the kitchen island.

Gemma giggles as though this is the best day of her life. Paisley jumps a little, then smiles and juts out her chin. Then my eyes turn to Tana, grinning as though she couldn't possibly be happier.

"It wasn't *my* idea," Paisley objects and shakes her head, backing up a step to distance herself. "They're the ones who decided to bring it home. You know I don't like cleaning up *poop*." She shudders at the mere thought.

I cross the kitchen to Tana's side and press a kiss to her temple. The cinnamon-sugar scent of her fills my nose, releasing any lingering tension I have from the never-ending arson investigation. Her body loosens in response and molds to mine. Her hand comes up to clutch at the shirt covering my stomach, and she pulls me close enough to kiss me firmly on the lips.

I'm forever grateful for the years we shared before the accident. A part of me will always miss the woman she used to be. But I love this version of her just as much. When she pulls me to her like this and kisses me as though she can't wait another moment, it reminds me every time how precious our life is together, how cherished. When she lingers against my lips, I know she senses it, too.

We only split up because Gemma giggles, and Paisley makes gagging sounds. "Can you guys, like, not?" Paisley asks and mimes sticking her finger down her throat. But I don't miss the way her lips turn to a smile when she goes to the fridge for a juice. Much as she likes to complain about everything in typical pre-teen fashion, Paisley couldn't be happier to have her family back together. In fact, the only reason I'd start to worry was if her moaning and complaining stopped.

Tana giggles and presses her lips more firmly against mine, making theatrical smacking sounds and causing Gemma to cackle even more.

"Ugh," Paisley says. "I'm going to my room. You guys are so gross."

I ruffle Gemma's hair and say to Tana, "So what did you bring home this time, sweet pea?"

"We found an orphaned squirrel baby at school today. I'm going to keep it here overnight until I can take it to Penny in the morning."

"A squirrel, huh? That's a first."

"Can I take it to its cage?" Paisley asks. "I'll be really careful, I promise."

Tana passes the creature over to Paisley, who lovingly whispers to it as she and Gemma leave the room.

"We're going to need a bigger house," I say to Tana once we're alone.

She makes a face. "I don't think so. We don't have *that* many animals. Besides, we're only fostering some of them, and some are just rehabbing until they get better. I won't bring home any more if you really—"

I shut her up with a finger over her lips. "I don't mean *those* animals." I put my other hand over her still flat stomach. "I mean this one. We need more room with another baby on the way."

"No, we don't. I told you that before. Besides, I like it here. We've been here a long time, and the girls love it. I don't want to uproot them."

"Baby, you're going to want more room. You don't want Gemma and Paisley sharing a room, do you?" I shudder. "Zeke's friend Malcolm is selling his place. It's in the country with a big yard for plenty of rescues. I'm just sayin'."

"Are you trying to bribe me?" Tana asks with narrowed eyes.

"Maybe. If this baby is another girl, I'm going to need all the space I can get. Are you sure you don't want to find out until they're born?"

She nods. "Positive. Are you ready to tell the girls yet? We can't keep it a secret forever."

"I'm ready if you are, sweet pea."

Tana pushes up on her toes to kiss me. "As long as you're with me, I'm ready for anything."

Continue the Battleboro Fire & Rescue Series with…
Saving His Heart!

ACKNOWLEDGMENTS

To the girl who spent her childhood buried in books, thank you for never giving up. For following your dreams.

To my mom, the best mother in the whole world. You're always there when I need you, no matter what. I love you to the moon and back.

Afton and Charlotte, I hope you're not reading this HAHA. I appreciate you for inspiring me to always do better, work harder. I wouldn't be where I am if it weren't for you both.

To Charlie. Always! Life with you is better than books.

A huge thank you to the girls in Nicole's Knockouts for motivating me each day to keep working and writing. I can't tell you how much it means to me to have you in my corner.

To the team who bring a book from production to publication including, but not limited to, IndieSage PR, editor Emily A. Lawrence, and the countless book bloggers and bookstagrammers THANK YOU!

ABOUT NICOLE BLANCHARD

Nicole Blanchard is the *New York Times* and *USA Today* best-selling author of dangerous romance from antiheroes to aliens. She and her family reside in the south along with menagerie of animals. Visit her website www.authornicoleblanchard.com for signed paperbacks, free books, and more!

ALSO BY NICOLE BLANCHARD

Battleboro Fire & Rescue Series

Storming His Heart

Shielding His Heart

Saving His Heart

First to Fight Series

Anchor

Warrior

Valor

Box Set: Books 1-3

Survivor

Savior

Honor

Box Set: Books 4-6

Traitor

Operator

Aviator

Captor

Protector

Armor

Friend Zone Series

Friend Zone

Frenemies

Friends with Benefits

Box Set

The Lost Planet Series

The Forgotten Commander

The Vanished Specialist

The Mad Lieutenant

Journey to the Lost Planet (Books 1-3)

The Uncertain Scientist

The Lonely Orphan

The Rogue Captain

Return to the Lost Planet (Books 4-6)

The Determined Hero

The Arrogant Genius

The Runaway Alien

Saving the Lost Planet (Books 7-9)

Dark Romance

Toxic

An Immortal Fairy Tale Series

Deal with the Dragon

Standalone Novellas

Bear with Me

Darkest Desires

Mechanical Hearts

www.ingramcontent.com/pod-product-compliance
Lightning Source LLC
Chambersburg PA
CBHW070458300726
48975CB00007B/2231